I0764484

THE MAN WHO BRIDGED THE MIST

a novella by

KIJ JOHNSON

PHOENIX PICK BOOKLETS

an imprint of

Rockville, Maryland

This story first appeared in *Asimov's*, October/November 2011.

ISBN: 978-1-61242-119-3

ISBN: 978-1-64973-031-2

Published by Phoenix Pick
an imprint of Arc Manor
P. O. Box 10339
Rockville, MD 20849-0339
www.ArcManor.com

Kit came to Nearside with two trunks and an oiled-cloth folio full of plans for the bridge across the mist. His trunks lay tumbled like stones at his feet where the mailcoach guard had dropped them. The folio he held close, away from the drying mud of yesterday's storm.

Nearside was small, especially to a man of the capital where buildings towered seven and eight stories tall, a city so large that even a vigorous walker could not cross in a day. Here hard-packed dirt roads threaded through irregular spaces scattered with structures and fences. Even the inn was plain, two stories of golden limestone and blue slate tiles with (he could smell) some sort of animals living behind it. On the sign overhead, a flat, pale blue fish very like a ray curvetted against a black background.

A brightly dressed woman stood by the inn's door. Her skin and eyes were pale, almost colorless. "Excuse me," Kit said. "Where can I find the ferry to take me across the mist?" He could feel himself being weighed, but amiably: a stranger, small and very dark, in gray—a man from the east.

The woman smiled. "Well, the ferries are both on this side, at the upper dock. But I expect what you really want is someone to oar the ferry, yes? Rasali Ferry came over from Farside last night. She's the one you'll want to talk to. She spends a lot of time at The Deer's Hart. But you wouldn't like The Hart, sir," she added. "It's not nearly as nice as The Fish here. Are you looking for a room?"

"I hope I'll be staying in Farside tonight," Kit said apologetically. He didn't want to seem arrogant. The invisible web of connections he would need for his work started here with this first impression, with all the first impressions of the next few days.

"That's what *you* think," the woman said. "I'm guessing it'll be a day or two—or more—before Rasali goes back. Valo Ferry might, but he doesn't cross so often."

"I could buy out the trip's fares, if that's why she's waiting."

"It's not that," the woman said. "She won't cross the mist 'til she's ready. "Until she feels it's right, if you follow me. But you can ask, I suppose."

Kit didn't follow but he nodded anyway. "Where's The Deer's Hart?"

She pointed. "Left, then right, then down by the little boat yard."

"Thank you," Kit said. "May I leave my trunks here until I work things out with her?"

"We always stow for travelers." The woman grinned. "And cater to them too, when they find out there's no way across the mist today."

The Deer's Hart was smaller than The Fish, and livelier. At midday the oak-shaded tables in the beer garden beside the inn were clustered with light-skinned people in brilliant clothes, drinking and tossing comments over the low fence into the boat yard next door where, half lost in steam, a youth and two women bent planks to form the hull of a small flat-bellied boat. When Kit spoke to a man carrying two mugs of something that looked like mud and smelled of yeast, the man gestured at the yard with his chin. "Ferrys are over there. Rasali's the one in red," he said as he walked away.

"The one in red" was tall, her skin as pale as that of the rest of the locals, with a black braid so long that she had looped it around her neck to keep it out of the way. Her shoulders flexed in the sunlight as she and the youth forced a curved plank to take the skeletal hull's shape and clamped it in place. The other woman, slightly shorter, with the ash-blond hair so common here, forced an augur through the plank and into a rib, then hammered a peg into the hole she'd made. After three pegs the boatwrights straightened. The plank held. *Strong,* Kit thought. *I wonder if I can get them for the bridge?*

"Rasali!" a voice bellowed, almost in Kit's ear. "Man here's looking for you." Kit turned in time to see the man with the mugs gesturing, again with his chin. He sighed and walked to the waist-high fence. The boatwrights stopped to drink from blueware bowls before the one in red and the youth came over.

"I'm Rasali Ferry of Farside," the woman said. Her voice was softer and higher than he had expected of a woman as strong as she, with the fluid vowels of the local accent. She nodded to the boy beside her: "Valo Ferry of Farside, my brother's eldest." Valo was more a young man than a boy, lighter-haired than Rasali and slightly taller. They had the same heavy eyebrows and direct amber eyes.

"Kit Meinem of Atyar," Kit said.

Valo asked, "What sort of name is Meinem? It doesn't mean anything."

"In the capital, we take our names differently than you."

"Oh, like Jenner Ellar." Valo nodded. "I guessed you were from the capital—your clothes and your skin."

Rasali said, "What can we do for you, Kit Meinem of Atyar?"

"I need to get to Farside today," Kit said.

Rasali shook her head. "I can't take you. I just got here and it's too soon. Perhaps Valo?"

The youth tipped his head to one side, his expression suddenly abstract. He shook his head. "No, not today, I don't think."

"I can buy out the fares if that helps. It's Jenner Ellar I am here to see."

Valo looked interested but said, "No," to Rasali, and she added, "What's so important that it can't wait a few days?"

Better now than later, Kit thought. "I am replacing Teniant Planner as the lead engineer and architect for construction of the bridge over the mist. We start work again as soon as I've reviewed everything. And had a chance to talk to Jenner." He watched their faces.

Rasali said, "It's been a year since Teniant died. I was starting to think Empire had forgotten all about us and that your deliveries would be here 'til the iron rusted away."

Valo frowned. "Jenner Ellar's not taking over?"

"The new Department of Roads cartel is in my name," Kit said, "but I hope Jenner will remain as my second. You can see why I would like to meet him as soon as is possible, of course. He will—"

Valo burst out, "You're going to take over from Jenner after he's worked so hard on this? And what about us? What about *our* work?" His cheeks were flushed an angry red. *How do they conceal anything with skin like that?* Kit thought.

"Valo," Rasali said, a warning tone in her voice. Flushing darker still, the youth turned and strode away. Rasali snorted but said only: "Boys. He likes Jenner and he has problems with the bridge, anyway."

That was worth addressing. *Later.* "So what will it take to get you to carry me across the mist, Rasali Ferry of Farside? The project will pay anything reasonable."

"I cannot," she said. "Not today, not tomorrow. You'll have to wait."

"Why?" Kit asked, reasonably enough, he thought; but she eyed him for a long moment as though deciding whether to be annoyed.

"Have you gone across mist before?" she said at last.

"Of course," he said.

"But not the river," she said.

"Not the river," he agreed. "It's a quarter-mile across here, yes?"

"Yes." She smiled suddenly, white even teeth and warmth like sunlight in her eyes. "Let's go down and perhaps I can explain things better there." She jumped the fence with a single powerful motion, landing beside him to a chorus of cheers and shouts from the garden's patrons. She slapped hands with one, then gestured to Kit to follow her. She was well liked, clearly. Her opinion would matter.

The boat yard was heavily shaded by low-hanging oaks and chestnuts, and bounded on the east by an open-walled shelter filled with barrels and stacks of lumber. Rasali waved at the third boat maker, who was still putting her tools away. "Tilisk Boatwright of Nearside. My brother's wife," she said to Kit. "She makes skiffs with us but she won't ferry. She's not born to it as Valo and I are."

"Where's your brother?" Kit asked.

"Dead," Rasali said and lengthened her stride.

They walked a few streets over and then climbed a long even ridge perhaps eighty feet high, too regular to be natural. *A levee,* Kit thought, and distracted himself from the steep path by estimating the volume of earth and the labor that had been required to build it. Decades, perhaps, but how long ago? How many miles did it stretch? Which department had overseen it, or had it been the locals? The levee was treeless. The only feature was a slender wood tower hung with flags on the ridge, probably for signaling across the mist to Farside since it appeared too fragile for anything else. They had storms out here, Kit knew; there'd been one the night before. How often was the tower struck by lightning?

Rasali stopped. "There."

Kit had been watching his feet. He looked up and nearly cried out as light lanced his suddenly tearing eyes. He fell back a step and shielded his face. What had blinded him was an immense band of mist reflecting the morning sun.

Kit had never seen the mist river itself, though he bridged mist before this, two simple post-and-beam structures over narrow gorges closer to the capital. From his work in Atyar, he knew what was to be known. It was not water nor anything like. It formed somehow in the deep gorge of the great riverbed before him. It found its way some hundreds of miles north, upstream through a hundred narrowing mist creeks and streams before failing at last in shreds of drying foam that left bare patches of earth where they collected.

The mist stretched to the south as well, a deepening, thickening band that poured out at last from the river's mouth a thousand miles south, to form the mist ocean, which lay on the face of the salt-water ocean. Water had to follow the river's bed to run somewhere beneath or through the mist, but there was no way to prove this.

There was mist nowhere but this river and its streams and sea, but the mist split Empire in half.

After a moment, the pain in Kit's eyes grew less and he opened them again. The river was a quarter-mile across where they stood, a great gash of light between the levees. It seemed nearly featureless, blazing under the sun like a river of cream or of bleached silk, but as his eyes accustomed themselves, he saw the surface was not smooth but heaped and hollowed, and that it shifted slowly, almost indiscernibly, as he watched.

Rasali stepped forward and Kit started. "I'm sorry," he said with a laugh. "How long have I been staring? It's just—I had no idea."

"No one does," Rasali said. Her eyes when he met them were amused.

The east and west levees were nearly identical, each treeless and scrub-covered, with a signal tower. The levee on their side ran down to a narrow bare bank half a dozen yards wide. There was a wooden dock and a boat ramp, a rough switchback leading down to them. Two large boats had been pulled onto the bank. Another, smaller dock was visible a hundred yards downstream, attended by a clutter of boats, sheds and indeterminate piles covered in tarps.

"Let's go down." Rasali led the way, her words coming back to him over her shoulder. "The little ferry is Valo's. *Pearlfinder. The Tranquil Crossing*'s mine." Her voice warmed when she said the name. "Eighteen feet long, eight wide. Mostly pine, but a purpleheart keel and pearwood headpiece. You can't see it from here, but the hull's sheathed in blue-dyed fishskin. I can carry three horses or a ton and a half of cartage or fifteen passengers. Or various combinations. I once carried twenty-four hunting dogs and two handlers. Never again."

Channeled by the levees, a steady light breeze eased down from the north. The air had a smell, not unpleasant but a little sour, wild. "How can you manage a boat like this alone? Are you that strong?"

"It's as big as I can handle," she said. "but Valo helps sometimes for really unwieldy loads. You don't paddle through mist. I mostly just coax the *Crossing* to where I want it to go. Anyway, the bigger the boat, the more likely that the Big Ones will notice it—though if you *do* run into a fish, the smaller the boat, the easier it is to swamp. Here we are."

They stood on the bank. The mist streams he had bridged had not prepared him for anything like this. Those were tidy little flows, more like fog collecting in hollows than this. From this angle, the river no longer seemed a smooth flow of creamy whiteness, nor even gently heaped clouds. The mist forced itself into hillocks and hollows, tight slopes perhaps twenty feet high that folded into one another. It had a surface but it was irregular, cracked in places and translucent in others. The boundary didn't seem as clearly defined as that between water and air.

"How can you move on this?" Kit said, fascinated. "Or even float?" The hillock immediately before them was flattening as he watched. Beyond it something like a vale stretched out for a few dozen yards before turning and becoming lost to his eyes.

"Well, I can't, not today," Rasali said. She sat on the gunwale of her boat, one leg swinging, watching him. "I can't push the *Crossing* up those slopes or find a safe path unless I feel it. If I went today, I know—I *know*—" she tapped her belly—"that I would find myself stranded on a pinnacle or lost in a hole. *That's* why I can't take you today, Kit Meinem of Atyar."

When Kit was a child, he had not been good with other people. He was small and easy to tease or ignore, and then he was sick for much of his seventh year and had to leave his crèche before the usual time, to convalesce in his mother's house. None of the children of the crèche came to visit him but he didn't mind that. He had books and puzzles, and whole quires of blank paper that his mother didn't mind him defacing.

The clock in the room in which he slept didn't work, so one day he used his penknife to take it apart. He arranged the wheels and cogs and springs in neat rows on the quilt in his room, by type and then by size; by materials; by weight; by shape.

He liked holding the tiny pieces, thinking of how they might have been formed and how they worked together. The patterns they made were interesting but he knew the best pattern would be the working one, when they were all put back into their right places and the clock performed its task again. He had to think that the clock would be happier that way, too.

He tried to rebuild the clock before his mother came upstairs from her counting house at the end of the day, but when he had reassembled things, there remained a pile of unused parts and it still didn't work; so he shut the clock up and hoped she wouldn't notice that it wasn't ticking. Four days more of trying things during the day and concealing his failures at night, and on the fifth day the clock started again. One piece hadn't fit anywhere, a small brass cog. Kit still carried that cog in his pen case.

Late that afternoon, Kit returned to the river's edge. It was hotter and the mud had dried to cracked dust. The air smelled like old rags left too long in a pail. He saw no one at the ferry dock, but at the fisher's dock upstream people were gathering, a score or more of men and women with children running about.

The clutter looked even more disorganized as he approached. The fishing boats were fat coracles fashioned of leather stretched on frames, all tipped bottom up to the sun and looking like giant warts. The mist had dropped so that he could see a band of exposed rock below the bank. He could see the dock's pilings clearly. They were not vertical but had been set at an angle to make a cantilevered deck braced into the stone underlying the bank. The wooden pilings had been sheathed in metal.

He approached a silver-haired woman doing something with a treble hook as long as her hand. "What are you catching with that?" he said.

Her forehead was wrinkled when she looked up, but she smiled when she saw him. "Oh, you're a stranger. From Atyar, dressed like that. Am I right? We catch fish—" Still holding the hook, she extended her arms as far as they would stretch. "Bigger than that, some of them. Looks like more storms, so they're going to be biting tonight. I'm Meg Threehooks. Of Nearside, obviously."

"Kit Meinem of Atyar. I take it you can't find a bottom?" He pointed to the pilings.

Meg Threehooks followed his glance. "It's there somewhere, but it's a long way down and we can't sink pilings because the mist dissolves the wood. Oh, and fish eat it. Same thing with our ropes, the boats, us—anything but metal and rock, really." She knotted a line around the hook's eye. The cord was dark and didn't look heavy enough for anything Kit could imagine catching on hooks that size.

"What are these made of, then?" He squatted to look at the framing under one of the coracles.

"Careful, that one's mine," Meg said. "The hides—well, and all the ropes—are fishskin. Mist fish, not water-fish. Tanning takes off some of the slime so they don't last forever either, not if they're afloat." She made a face. "We have a saying: foul as fish-slime. That's pretty nasty, you'll see."

"I need to get to Farside," Kit said. "Could I hire you to carry me across?"

"In my boat?" She snorted. "No, fishers stay close to shore. Go see Rasali Ferry. Or Valo."

"I saw her," he said ruefully.

"Thought so. You must be the new architect—city folk are always so impatient. You're so eager to be dinner for a Big One? If Rasali doesn't want to go then don't go, stands to reason."

Kit was footsore and frustrated by the time he returned to The Fish. His trunks were already upstairs, in a small cheerful room overwhelmed by a table that nearly filled it, with a stiflingly hot cupboard bed. When Kit spoke to the woman he'd talked to earlier, Brana Keep, the owner of The Fish (its real name turned out to be The Big One's Delight) laughed. "Rasali's as hard to shift as bedrock," she said. "And truly, you would not be comfortable at The Hart."

By the next morning, when Kit came downstairs to break his fast on flatbread and pepper-rubbed water-fish, everyone appeared to know everything about him, especially his task. He had wondered whether there would be resistance to the project, but if there had been any it was gone now. There were a few complaints, mostly about slow payments—a universal issue for public works—but none at all about the labor or organization. Most in the taproom seemed not to mind the bridge, and the feeling everywhere he went in town was optimistic. He'd run into more resistance elsewhere, building smaller bridges.

"Well, why should we be concerned?" Brana Keep said to Kit. "You're bringing in people to work, yes? So we'll be selling room and board and clothes and beer to them. And you'll be hiring some of us and everyone will do well while you're building this bridge of yours. I plan to be wading ankle-deep through gold by the time this is done."

"And after," Kit said, "when the bridge is complete—think of it, the first real link between the east and west sides of Empire. The only place for three thousand miles where people and trade can cross the mist easily, safely, whenever they wish. You'll be the heart of Empire in ten years. Five." He laughed a little, embarrassed by the passion that shook his voice.

"Yes, well," Brana Keep said in the easy way of a woman who makes her living by not antagonizing customers, "we'll make that harness when the colt is born."

For the next six days, Kit explored the town and surrounding countryside.

He met the masons, a brother and sister that Teniant had selected before her death to oversee the pillar and anchorage construction on Nearside. They were quiet but competent and Kit was comfortable not replacing them.

Kit also spoke with the Nearside ropemakers, and performed tests on their fishskin ropes and cables, which turned out even stronger than he had hoped, with excellent resistance to rot and to catastrophic and slow failure. The makers told him that the rope stretched for its first two years in use, which made it ineligible to replace the immense chains that would bear the bridge's weight; but it could replace the thousands of vertical suspender chains that would support the roadbed with a great saving in weight.

He spent much of his time watching the mist. It changed character unpredictably: a smooth rippled flow, hours later a badland of shredding foam, still later a field of steep dunes that joined and shifted as he watched. The river generally dropped in its bed each day under the sun and rose after dark, though it wasn't consistent.

The winds were more predictable. Hedged between the levees, they streamed southward each morning and northward each evening, growing stronger toward midday and dusk, and falling away entirely in the afternoons and at night. They did not seem to affect the mist much except for tearing off shreds that landed on the banks as dried foam.

The winds meant that there would be more dynamic load on the bridge than Teniant Planner had predicted. Kit would never criticize her work publicly and he gladly acknowledged her brilliant interpersonal skills, which had brought the town into cheerful collaboration, but he was grateful that her bridge had not been built as designed.

He examined the mist more closely, as well, by lifting a piece from the river's surface on the end of an oar. The mist was stiffer than it looked, and in bright light he thought he could see tiny shapes, perhaps creatures or plants or something altogether different. There were microscopes in Atyar, and people who studied these things; but he had never bothered to learn more, interested only in the structure that would bridge it. In any case, living things interested him less than structures.

Nights, Kit worked on the table in his room. Teniant's plans had to be revised. He opened the folios and cases she had left behind and read everything he found there. He wrote letters, wrote lists, wrote schedules, wrote duplicates of everything, sent to the capital for someone to do all the subsequent copying. His new plans for the bridge began to take shape. He started to glimpse the invisible architecture that was the management of the vast project.

He did not see Rasali Ferry except to ask each morning whether they might travel that day. The answer was always no.

One afternoon, when the clouds were heaping into anvils filled with rain, he walked up to the building site half a mile north of Nearside. For two years, off and on, carts had tracked south on the Hoic Mine road and the West River Road, leaving limestone blocks and iron bars here in untidy heaps. Huge dismantled shear-legs lay beside a caretaker's wattle-and-daub hut. There were thousands of large rectangular blocks.

Kit examined some of the blocks. Limestone was often too chossy for large-scale construction but this rock was sound, with no apparent flaws or fractures. There were not enough, of course, but undoubtedly more had been quarried. He had written to order resumption of deliveries and they would start arriving soon.

Delivered years too early, the iron trusses that would eventually support the roadbed were stacked neatly, painted black to protect them from moisture, covered in oiled tarps, and raised from the ground on planks. Sheep grazed the knee-high grass that grew everywhere. When one eyed him incuriously, Kit found himself bowing. "Forgive the intrusion," he said and laughed: too old to be talking to sheep.

The test pit was still open, with a ladder on the ground nearby. Weeds clung when he moved the ladder as though reluctant to release it. He descended.

The pasture had not been noisy but he was startled when he dropped below ground level and the insects and whispering grasses were suddenly silenced. The soil around him was striated shades of dun and dull yellow. Halfway down, he sliced a wedge free with his knife: lots of clay, good foundation soil as he had been informed. Some twenty feet down, the pit's bottom looked like the walls, but when he crouched to dig at the dirt between his feet with his knife, he hit rock almost immediately. It seemed to be shale. He wondered how far down the water table was. Did the Nearsiders find it difficult to dig wells? Did the mist ever backwash into one? There were people at University in Atyar who were trying to understand mist, but there was still so much that could not be examined or quantified.

He collected a rock to examine in better light and climbed from the pit in time to see a teamster approaching, leading four mules, her wagon groaning under the weight of the first new blocks. A handful of Nearsider men and women followed, rolling their shoulders and popping their joints. They called out greetings and he walked across to them.

When he got back to The Fish hours later, exhausted from helping unload the cart and soaked from the storm that had started while he did so, there was a message from Rasali. *Dusk* was all it said.

Kit was stiff and irritable when he left for *The Tranquil Crossing*. He had hired a carrier from The Fish to haul one of his trunks down to the dock but the others remained in his room, which he would probably keep until the bridge was done. He carried his folio of plans and paperwork himself. He was leaving duplicates of everything on Nearside, but after so much work it was hard to trust any of it to the hands of others.

The storm was over and the clouds were moving past, leaving the sky every shade between lavender and a rich purple-blue. The largest moon was a crescent in the west, the smaller a half circle immediately overhead. In the fading light, the mist was a dark, smoky streak. The air smelled fresh. Kit's mood lightened and he half-trotted down the final slope.

His fellow passengers were there before him: a prosperous-looking man with a litter of piglets in a woven wicker cage (Tengon whites, the man confided, the best bloodline in all Empire); a woman in the dark clothes fashionable in the capital, with brass-bound document cases and a folio very like Kit's; two traders with many cartons of powdered pigment; a mail courier with locked leather satchels and two guards. Nervous about their first crossing, Uni and Tom Mason greeted Kit when he arrived.

In the gathering darkness the mist formed tight-folded hills and coulees. Swifts darted just above the surface, using the wind flowing up the valley, searching for insects, he supposed. Once a sudden black shape, too quick to see clearly, appeared from below. Then it, and one of the birds, was gone.

The voices of the fishers at their dock carried to him. They launched their boats and he watched one and then another and then a gaggle of the little coracles push themselves up a slope of the mist. There were no lamps.

"Ready, everyone?" Kit had not heard Rasali approach. She swung down into the ferry. "Hand me your gear."

Stowing and embarkation were quick, though the piglets complained. Kit strained his eyes but the coracles could no longer be seen. When he noticed Rasali waiting for him, he apologized. "I guess the fish are biting."

Rasali glanced at the river as she stowed his trunk. "Small ones. A couple of feet long only. The fishers like them bigger, five or six feet, though they don't want them too big, either. But they're not fish, not what you think fish are. Hand me that."

He hesitated a moment, then gave her the folio before stepping into the ferry. *The Tranquil Crossing* sidled at his weight but sluggishly: a carthorse instead of a riding mare. His stomach lurched. "Oh!" he said.

"What?" one of the traders asked nervously. Rasali untied the rope holding them, pulled it into the boat.

Kit swallowed. "I had forgotten. The motion of the boat. It's not like water at all."

He did not mention his fear but there was no need. The others murmured assent. The courier, her dark face sharp-edged as a hawk, growled, "Every time I do this, it surprises me. I dislike it."

Rasali unshipped a scull and slid the great triangular blade into the mist, which parted reluctantly. "I've been on mist more than water but I remember the way water felt. Quick and jittery. This is better."

"Only to you, Rasali Ferry," Uni Mason said.

"Water's safer, anyway," the man with the piglets said.

Rasali leaned into the oar and the boat slid away from the dock. "Anything is safe until it kills you."

The mist absorbed the quiet sounds of shore almost immediately. One of Kit's first projects had been a stone single-arch bridge over water, far to the north in Eskje province. He had visited before construction started, and he was there for five days more than he had expected, caught by a snowstorm that left nearly two feet on the ground. This reminded him of those snowy moonless nights, the air as thick and silencing as a pillow on the ears.

Rasali did not scull so much as steer. It was hard to see far in any direction except up, but perhaps it was true that the mist spoke to her for she seemed to know where best to position the boat for the mist to carry it forward. She followed a small valley until it started to flatten and then mound up. The *Crossing* tipped slightly as it slid a few feet to port. The mail carrier made a noise and immediately stifled it.

Mist was a misnomer. It was denser than it seemed. Sometimes the boat seemed not to move through it so much as across its surface. Tonight it seemed like the dirty foam that strong winds could whip from Churash Lake's waves, near the western coast of Empire. Kit reached a hand over the boat's side. The mist piled against his hand, almost dry to the touch, sliding up his forearm with a sensation he could not immediately identify. When he realized it was prickling, he snatched his arm back in and rubbed it on a fold of his coat. The skin burned. Caustic, of course.

The man with the pigs whispered, "Will they come if we talk or make noise?"

"Not to talking or pigs' squealing," Rasali said. "They seem to like low noises. They'll rise to thunder sometimes."

One of the traders said, "What are they if they're not really fish? What do they look like?" Her voice shook. The mist was weighing on them all, all but Rasali.

"If you want to know you'll have to see one for yourself," Rasali said. "Or try to get a fisher to tell you. They gut and fillet them over the sides of their boats. No one else sees much but meat wrapped in paper or rolls of black skin for the ropemakers and tanners."

"*You've* seen them," Kit said.

"They're broad and flat. But ugly."

"And Big Ones?" Kit asked.

Her voice was harsh. "*Them* we don't talk about here."

No one spoke for a time. Mist—foam—heaped up at the boat's prow and parted, eased to the sides with an almost inaudible hissing. Once the mist off the port side heaved and something dark broke the surface for a moment, followed by other dark somethings, but they were not close enough to see well. One of the merchants cried without a sound or movement.

The Farside levee showed at last, a black mass that didn't get any closer for what felt like hours. Fighting his fear, Kit leaned over the side, keeping his face away from the surface. "It can't really be bottomless," he said half to himself. "What's under it?"

"You wouldn't hit the bottom, anyway," Rasali said.

The Tranquil Crossing eased up a long swell of mist and into a hollow. Rasali pointed the ferry along a crease. And then they were suddenly a stone's throw from the Farside dock and the light of its torches.

People on the dock moved as they approached. Just loudly enough to carry, a soft baritone voice called, "Rasali?"

She called back, "Ten this time, Pen."

"Anyone need carriers?" A different voice. Several passengers responded.

Rasali shipped the scull while the ferry was still some feet away from the dock, and allowed it to ease forward under its own momentum. She stepped to the prow and picked up a coiled rope there, tossing one end across the narrowing distance. Someone on the dock caught it and pulled the boat in, and in a very few moments the ferry was snug against the dock.

Disembarking and payment was quicker than embarkation had been. Kit was the last off and after a brief discussion he hired a carrier to haul his trunk to an inn in town. He turned to say farewell to Rasali. She and the man—Pen, Kit remembered—were untying the boat. "You're not going back already," he said.

"Oh, no." Her voice sounded loose, content, relaxed. Kit hadn't known how tense she was. "We're just going to tow the boat down to where the Twins will pull it out." She waved with one hand to the boat launch. A pair of white oxen gleamed in the night, at their heads a woman hardly darker.

"Wait," Kit said to Uni Mason and handed her his folio. "Please tell the innkeeper I'll be there soon." He turned back to Rasali. "May I help?"

In the darkness he felt more than saw her smile. "Always."

The Red Lurcher, more commonly called The Bitch, was a small but noisy inn five minutes' walk from the mist, ten (he was told) from the building site. His room was larger than at The Fish, with an uncomfortable bed and a window seat crammed with quires of ancient hand-written music. Jenner stayed here, Kit knew, but when he asked the owner (Widson Innkeep, a heavyset man with red hair turning silver), he had not seen him. "You'll be the new one, the architect," Widson said.

"Yes," Kit said. "When he gets in, please tell Jenner I am here."

Widson wrinkled his forehead. "I don't know, he's been out late most days recently, since—" He cut himself off, looking guilty.

"—since the signals informed him that I was here," Kit said. "I understand the impulse."

The innkeeper seemed to consider something for a moment, then said slowly, "We like Jenner here."

"Then we'll try to keep him," Kit said.

When the child Kit had recovered from his illness, he did not return to the crèche—which he would have been leaving in a year in any case—but went straight to his father. Davell Meinem was a slow-talking humorous man who nevertheless had a sharp tongue on the sites of his many projects. He brought Kit with him to his work places: best for the boy to get some experience in the trade.

Kit loved everything about his father's projects: the precisely drawn plans, the orderly progression of construction, the lines and curves of brick and iron and stone rising under the endlessly random sky.

For the first year or two, Kit imitated his father and the workers, building structures of tiny beams and bricks made by the woman set to mind him, a tiler who had lost a hand some years back. Davell collected the boy at the end of the day. "I'm here to inspect the construction," he said, and Kit demonstrated his bridge or tower, or the materials he had laid out in neat lines and stacks. Davell would discuss Kit's work with great seriousness until it grew too dark to see and they went back to the inn or rented rooms that passed for home near the sites.

Davell spent nights buried in the endless paperwork of his projects, and Kit found this interesting as well. The pattern that went into building something big was not just the architectural plans or the construction itself; it was also labor schedules and documentation and materials deliveries. He started to draw his own plans but he also made up endless correspondences with imaginary providers.

After a while, Kit noticed that a large part of the pattern that made a bridge or a tower was built of people.

The knock on Kit's door came very late that night, a preemptory rap. Kit put down the quill he was mending and rolled his shoulders to loosen them. "Yes," he said aloud as he stood.

The man who stormed through the door was as dark as Kit, though perhaps a few years younger. He wore mud-splashed riding clothes.

"I am Kit Meinem of Atyar," Kit said.

"Jenner Ellar of Atyar. Show it to me." Silently Kit handed the cartel to Jenner, who glared at it before tossing it onto the table. "It took long enough for them to pick a replacement."

Might as well deal with this right now, Kit thought. "You hoped it would be you."

Jenner eyed Kit for a moment. "Yes. I did."

"You think you're the most qualified to complete the project because you've been here for the last—what is it? year?"

"I know the sites," Jenner said. "I worked with Teniant to make those plans. And then Empire sends—" He turned to face the empty hearth.

"—Empire sends someone new," Kit said to Jenner's back. "Someone with connections in the capital, influential friends but no experience with this site, this bridge. It should have been you, yes?"

Jenner was still.

"But it isn't," Kit said, and let the words hang for a moment. "I've built eight bridges in the past fifteen years. Four suspension bridges, two major spans. Two bridges over mist. You've done three, and the biggest span you've directed was three hundred and fifty feet, six stone arches over shallow water and shifting gravel on Mati River."

"I know," Jenner snapped.

"It's a good bridge." Kit poured two glasses of whiskey from a stoneware pitcher by the window. "I coached down to see it before I came here. It's well made and you were on budget and nearly on schedule in spite of the drought. Better, the locals still like you. Asked how you're doing these days. Here."

Jenner took the glass Kit offered. *Good.* Kit continued, "Meinems have built bridges—and roads and aqueducts and stadia, a hundred sorts of public structures—for Empire for a thousand years." Jenner turned to speak but Kit held up his hand. "This doesn't mean we're any better at it than Ellars. But Empire knows us—and we know Empire, how to do what we need to. If they'd given you this bridge, you'd be replaced within a year. But I can get this bridge built and I will." Kit sat and leaned forward, elbows on knees. "With you. You're talented. You know the site. You know the people. Help me make this bridge."

"It's real to you," Jenner said finally. Kit knew what he meant: *You care about this work. It's not just another tick on a list.*

"Yes," Kit said. "You'll be my second for this one. I'll show you how to deal with Atyar and I'll help you with contacts. And your next project will belong entirely to you. This is the first bridge but it isn't going to be the only one across the mist."

Together they drank. The whiskey bit at Kit's throat and made his eyes water. "Oh," he said, "that's *awful.*"

Jenner laughed suddenly and met his eyes for the first time: a little wary still but willing to be convinced. "Farside whiskey is terrible. You drink much of this, you'll be running for Atyar in a month."

"Maybe we'll have something better ferried across," Kit said.

Preparations were not so far along on this side. The heaps of blocks at the construction site were not so massive and it was harder to find local workers. In discussions between Kit, Jenner and the Near- and Farside masons who would oversee construction of the pillars, final plans materialized. This would be unique, the largest structure of its kind ever attempted: a single-span chain suspension bridge a quarter of a mile long. The basic plan remained unchanged: the bridge would be supported by eyebar-and-bolt chains, four on each side, allowed to play independently to compensate for the slight shifts that would be caused by traffic on the roadbed. The huge eyebars and their bolts were being fashioned five hundred miles away and far to the north, where iron was common and the smelting and ironworking were the best in Empire. Kit had just written to the foundries to start the work again.

The pillar and anchorage on Nearside would be built of gold limestone anchored with pilings into the bedrock; on Farside they would be pink-gray granite with a funnel-shaped foundation. The towers' heights would be nearly four hundred feet. There were taller towers back in Atyar, but none had to stand against the compression of a bridge.

The initial tests with the fishskin rope had showed it to be nearly as strong as iron without the weight. When Kit asked the Farside tanners and ropemakers about its durability, he was taken a day's travel east to Feknai, to a waterwheel that used knotted belts of the material for its drive. The belts, he was told, were seventy-five years old and still sound. Fishskin wore like maplewood so long as it wasn't left in mist, but it required regular maintenance.

He watched Feknai's little river for a time. There had been rain recently in the foothills and the water was quick and abrupt as light. *Water bridges are easy,* he thought a little wistfully, and then: *Anyone can bridge water.*

Kit revised the plans again to use the lighter material where they could. Jenner crossed the mist to Nearside to work with Daell and Stivvan Cabler on the expansion of their workshops and ropewalk.

Without Jenner (who was practically a local, as Kit was told again and again), Kit felt the difference in attitudes on the river's two banks more clearly. Most Farsiders shared the Nearsiders' attitudes—money is money and always welcome—and there was a sense of the excitement that comes of any great project, but there was more resistance here. Empire was effectively split by the river, and the lands to the east—starting with Nearside—had never seen their destinies as closely linked to Atyar in the west. They were overseen by the eastern capital, Triple, and their taxes went to building necessities on their own side of the mist. Empire's grasp on the eastern lands was loose and had never needed to be tighter.

The bridge would change things. Travel between Atyar and Triple would grow more common and perhaps Empire would no longer hold the eastern lands so gently. Triple's lack of enthusiasm for the project showed itself in delayed deliveries of stone and iron. Kit traveled five days along the Triple Road to the district seat to present his credentials to the governor, and wrote sharp letters to the Department of Roads in Triple. Things became a little easier.

It was midwinter before the design was finished. Kit avoided crossing the mist. Rasali Ferry crossed seventeen times. He managed to see her nearly every time, at least for as long as it took to drink a beer.

The second time Kit crossed, it was midmorning of an early spring day. The mist mirrored the overcast sky above: pale and flat, like a layer of fog in a dell. Rasali was loading the ferry at the upper dock when Kit arrived and to his surprise she smiled at him, her face suddenly beautiful. Kit nodded to the stranger watching Valo toss immense cloth-wrapped bales to Rasali, then greeted the Ferrys. Valo paused for a moment but did not return Kit's greeting, only bent again to his work. Valo had been avoiding him since the beginning of his time there. With a mental shrug, Kit turned from Valo to Rasali. She was catching and stacking the enormous bales easily.

"What's in those? You throw them as though they were—"

"—paper," she finished. "The very best Ibraric mulberry paper. Light as lambswool. You probably have a bunch of this stuff in that folio of yours."

Kit thought of the vellum he used for his plans, and the paper he used for everything else: made of cotton from the south, its surface buffed until it felt hard and smooth as enamelwork. Ibraric paper was only useful for certain kinds of printing. He said, "All the time."

Rasali piled on bales and more bales until the ferry was stacked three high. He added, "Is there going to be room for me in there?"

"Pilar Runner and Valo aren't coming with us," she said. "You'll have to sit on top of the bales, but there's room as long as you sit still and don't wobble."

As Rasali pushed away from the dock Kit asked, "Why isn't the trader coming with her paper?"

"Why would she? Pilar has a broker on the other side." Her hands busy, she tipped her head to one side in a gesture that somehow conveyed a shrug. "Mist is dangerous." Somewhere along the River a ferry was lost every few months: horses, people, cartage, all lost. Fishers stayed closer to shore and died less often. It was harder to calculate the impact to trade and communications of this barrier splitting Empire in half.

This journey—in daylight, alone with Rasali—was very different from Kit's earlier crossing: less frightening but somehow wilder, stranger. The cold wind down the river was cutting and brought bits of dried foam to rest on his skin, but they blew off quickly without pain and left no mark. The wind fell to a breeze and then to nothing as they navigated into the mist.

They moved through what looked like a layered maze of cirrus clouds. He watched the mist along the *Crossing*'s side until they passed over a small hole like a pockmark, straight down and no more than a foot across. For an instant he glimpsed open space below them. They were floating on a layer of mist above an air pocket deep enough to swallow the boat. He rolled onto his back to stare up at the sky until he stopped shaking; when he looked again, they were out of the maze, it seemed. The boat eased along a gently curving channel. He relaxed a little and moved to watch Rasali.

"How fares your bridge?" Rasali said at last, her voice muted in the muffled air. This had to be a courtesy—everyone in town seemed to know everything about the bridge's progress—but Kit was used to answering questions to which people already knew the answers. He had found patience to be a highly effective tool.

"Farside foundations are doing well. We have maybe six more months before the anchorage is done, but pilings for the pillar's foundation are in place and we can start building. Six weeks early," Kit said a little smugly, though this was a victory no one else would appreciate and in any case the weather was as much to be credited as any action on his part. "On Nearside, we've run into basalt that's too hard to drill easily so we sent for a specialist. The signal flags say she's arrived, and that's why I'm crossing."

She said nothing, seemingly intent on moving the great scull. He watched her for a time, content to see her shoulders flex, hear her breath forcing itself out in smooth waves. Over the faint yeast scent of the mist, he smelled her sweat, or thought he did. She frowned slightly but he could not tell whether it was due to her labor or something in the mist, or something else. Who was she, really? "May I ask a question, Rasali Ferry of Farside?"

Rasali nodded, eyes on the mist in front of the boat.

Actually, he had several things he wished to know: about her, about the river, about the people here. He picked one almost at random. "What is bothering Valo?"

"He's transparent, isn't he? He thinks you take something away from him," Rasali said. "He is too young to know what you take is unimportant."

Kit thought about it. "His work?"

"His work is unimportant?" She laughed, a sudden puff of an exhale as she pulled. "We have a lot of money, Ferrys. We own land and rent it out—The Deer's Hart belongs to my family; did you know that? But he's young and he wants what we all want at his age, a chance to test himself against the world and see if he measures up. And because he's a Ferry he wants be tested against adventures. Danger. The mist. Valo thinks you take that away from him."

"But he's not immortal," Kit said, "whatever he thinks. The river can kill him. It will, sooner or later. It—"

—will kill you. Kit caught himself, rolled onto his back again to look up at the sky.

In The Bitch's taproom one night, a local man had told him about Rasali's family: a history of deaths, of boats lost in a silent hissing of mist, or the rending of wood, or screams that might be human and might be a horse. "So everyone wears ash-color for a month or two, and then the next Ferry takes up the business. Rasali's still new, two years maybe. When she goes, it'll be Valo, then Valo's sister. Unless Rasali or Valo have kids by then.

"They're always beautiful," the man had added after some more porter, "the Ferrys. I suppose that's to make up for having such short lives."

Kit looked down from the paper bales at Rasali. "But you're different. You don't feel you're losing anything."

"You don't know what I feel, Kit Meinem of Atyar." Cool light moved along the muscles of her arms. Her voice came again, softer. "I am not young; I don't need to prove myself. But I will lose this. The mist, the silence."

Then tell me, he did not say. *Show me.*

She was silent for the rest of the trip. Kit thought perhaps she was angry, but when he invited her, she accompanied him to the building site.

The quiet pasture was gone. All that remained of the tall grass was struggling tufts and dirty straw. The air smelled of sweat and meat and the bitter scent of hot metal. There were more blocks here now, a lot more. The pits for the anchorage and the pillar were excavated to bedrock, overshadowed by mountains of dirt. One sheep remained, skinned and spitted, and greasy smoke rose as a boy turned it over a fire beside the temporary forge. Kit had considered the pasture a nuisance, but looking at the skewered sheep he felt a twinge of guilt.

The rest of the flock had been replaced by sturdy-looking women and men who were using rollers to shift stones down a dugout ramp into the hole for the anchorage foundation. Dust dulled their skin and muted the bright colors of their short kilts and breastbands. In spite of the cold, sweat had cleared tracks along their muscles.

One of the workers waved to Rasali and she waved back. Kit recalled his name: Mik Rounder, very strong but he needed direction. Had they been lovers? Relationships out here were tangled in ways Kit didn't understand. In the capital such things were more formal and often involved contracts.

Jenner and a small woman knelt conferring on the exposed stone floor of the larger pit. When Kit slid down the ladder to join them, the small woman bowed slightly. Her eyes and short hair and skin all seemed to be turning the same iron gray. "I am Liu Breaker of Hoic. Your specialist."

"Kit Meinem of Atyar. How shall we address this?"

"Your Jenner says you need some of this basalt cleared away, yes?"

Kit nodded.

Liu knelt to run her hand along the pit's floor. "See where the color and texture change along this line? Your Jenner was right: this upthrust of basalt is a problem. Here where the shale is, you can carve out most of the foundation the usual way with drills, picks. But the basalt is too hard to drill." She straightened and brushed dust from her knees. "Have you ever seen explosives used?"

Kit shook his head. "We haven't needed them for any of my projects. I've never been to the mines, either."

"Not much good anywhere else," Liu said, "but very useful for breaking up large amounts of rock. A lot of the blocks you have here were loosed using explosives." She grinned. "You'll like the noise."

"We can't afford to break the bedrock's integrity."

"I brought enough powder for a number of small charges. Comparatively small."

"How—"

Liu held up a weathered hand. "I don't need to understand bridges to walk across one. Yes?"

Kit laughed outright. "Yes."

Liu Breaker was right; Kit liked the noise very much. Liu would not allow anyone close to the pit but even from what she considered a safe distance, behind a huge pile of dirt, the explosion was an immense shattering thing, a crack of thunder that shook the earth. There was a second of echoing silence. After a collective gasp and some scattered screams, the workers cheered and stamped their feet. A small cloud of mingled smoke and rock dust eased over the pit's edge, sharp with the smell of saltpeter. The birds were not happy; with the explosion, they had burst from their trees and wheeled nervously.

Grinning, Liu climbed from her bunker near the pit, her face dust-caked everywhere but around her eyes, which had been protected by the wooden slit-goggles now hanging around her neck. "So far so good," she shouted over the ringing in Kit's ears. Seeing his face she laughed. "These are nothing—gnat sneezes. You should hear when we quarry granite up at Hoic."

Kit was going to speak more with her when he noticed Rasali striding away, toward the river. He had forgotten she was there. He followed her, half shouting to hear himself. "Some noise, yes?"

Rasali whirled. "What are you *thinking*?" She was shaking and her lips were white.

Taken aback, Kit answered, "We are blowing the foundations." *Rage? Fear?* He wished he could think a little more clearly but the sound seemed to have stunned his wits.

"And making the earth shake! The Big Ones come to thunder, Kit!"

"It wasn't thunder," he said.

"Tell me it wasn't worse!" Tears glittered in her eyes. Her voice was dulled by the drumming in his ears. "They will come, I *know* it."

He reached a hand out to her. "It's a tall levee, Rasali. Even if they do, they're not going to come over that." His heart in his chest thrummed. His head was hurting. It was so hard to hear her.

"*No one* knows what they'll do! They used to destroy whole towns, drifting inland on foggy nights. Why do you think they built the levees a thousand years ago? The Big Ones—"

She stopped shouting, listening. She mouthed something but Kit could not hear her over the beating in his ears, his heart, his head. He realized suddenly that these were not the after-effects of the explosion; the air itself was beating. He was aware at the edges of his vision of the other workers, every face turned toward the mist. There was nothing to see but the overcast sky. No one moved.

But the sky was moving.

Behind the levee the river mist was rising, a great boiling upheaval of dirty gray-gold against the steel-gray of the clouds, at least a hundred feet high, to be seen over the levee. The mist was seething, breaking open in great swirls and rifts, everything moving, changing. Kit had seen a great fire once when a warehouse of linen had burned in Atyar, where the smoke had poured upward and looked a little like this before being torn apart by the wind.

Gaps opened in the mountain of mist and closed, and others opened, darker the deeper they were. And through those gaps, in the brown-black shadows at the heart of the mist, was movement.

The gaps closed. After an eternity the mist slowly smoothed and then settled back behind the levee and could no longer be seen. He wasn't really sure when the thrumming of the air blended back into the ringing of his ears.

"Gone," Rasali said with a sound like a sob.

A worker made one of the vivid jokes that come after fear; the others laughed, too loud. A woman ran up the levee and shouted down, "Farside levees are fine; ours are fine." More laughter: people jogged off to Nearside to check on their families.

The back of Kit's hand was burning. A flake of foam had settled and left an irregular mark. "I only saw mist," Kit said. "Was there a Big One?"

Rasali shook herself, stern now but no longer angry or afraid. Kit had learned this about the Ferrys, that their emotions coursed through them and then dissolved. "It was in there. I've seen the mist boil like that before but never so big. Nothing else could heave it up like that."

"On purpose?"

"Oh, who knows? They're a mystery, the Big Ones." She met his eyes. "I hope your bridge is very high, Kit Meinem of Atyar."

Kit looked to where the mist had been, but there was only sky. "The deck will be two hundred feet above the mist. High enough. I hope."

Liu Breaker walked up to them, rubbing her hands on her leather leggings. "So, *that's* not something that happens at Hoic. *Very* exciting. What do you call that? How do we prevent it next time?"

Rasali looked at the smaller woman for a moment. "I don't think you can. Big Ones come when they come."

Liu said, "They do not always come?"

Rasali shook her head.

"Well, cold comfort is better than no comfort, as my Da says."

Kit rubbed his temples. The headache remained. "We'll continue."

"Then you'll have to be careful," Rasali said, "or you will kill us all."

"The bridge will save many lives," Kit said. *Yours, eventually.*

Rasali turned on her heel.

Kit did not follow her, not that day. Whether it was because subsequent explosions were smaller ("As small as they can be and earn my fees," Liu Breaker said) or because they were doing other things, the Big Ones did not return, though fish were plentiful for the three months it took to plan and plant the charges, and break the bedrock.

There was also a Meinem tradition of metal working, and Meinem reeves, and many Meinems went into fields altogether different, but Kit had known from nearly the beginning that he would be one of the building Meinems. He loved the invisible architecture of construction, looking for a compromise between the vision in his head and the sites, the materials, and the people that would make them real. The challenge was to compromise as little as possible.

Architecture was studied at University. His tutor was a materials specialist, a woman who had directed construction on an incredible twenty-three bridges. Skossa Timt was so old that her skin and hair had faded together to the white of Gani marble, and she walked with a cane she had designed herself for efficiency. She taught him much. Materials had rules, patterns of behavior: they bent or crumbled or cracked or broke under quantifiable stresses. They augmented or destroyed one another. Even the best materials in the most stable combinations did not last forever—she tapped her own forehead with one gnarled finger and laughed—but if he did his work right, they could last a thousand years or more. "But not forever," Skossa said. "Do your best but don't forget this."

The anchorages and pillars grew. Workers came from towns up and down each bank, and locals were hired on the spot. The new people were generally welcome. They paid for rooms and food and goods of all sorts. The taverns settled into making double and then triple batches of everything, threw out new wings and stables. Nearside accepted the new people easily, the only fights late at night when people had been drinking and flirting more than they should. Farside had fist fights more frequently, though they decreased steadily as skeptics gave in to the money that flowed into Farside, or to the bridge itself, its pillars too solid to be denied.

Farmers and husbanders sold their fields and new buildings sprawled out from the towns' hearts. Some were made of wattle and daub, slapped together over stamped-earth floors that still smelled of sheep dung. Others, small but permanent, went up more slowly, as the bridge builders laid fieldstones and timber in their evenings and on rest days.

The new people and locals mixed together until it was hard to tell the one from the other, though the older townfolk kept scrupulous track of who truly belonged. For those who sought lovers and friends, the new people were an opportunity to meet someone other than the men and women they had known since childhood. Many took casual lovers, and several term-partnered with new people. There was even a Nearside wedding, between Kes Tiler and a black-eyed builder from far to the south called Jolite Deveren, whatever that meant.

Kit did not have lovers. Working every night until he fell asleep over his paperwork, he didn't miss it much, except late on certain nights when thunderstorms left him restless and unnaturally alert, as though lightning ran under his skin. Some nights he thought of Rasali, wondered whether she was sleeping with someone that night or alone, and wondered if the storm had awakened her, left her restless as well.

Kit saw a fair amount of Rasali when they were both on the same side of the mist. She was clever and calm and the only person who did not want to talk about the bridge all the time.

He did not forget what Rasali said about Valo. Kit had been a young man himself not so many years before, and he remembered the hunger that young men and women felt to prove themselves against the world. Kit didn't need Valo to accept the bridge—he was scarcely into adulthood and his only influence over the townspeople was based on his work—but Kit liked the youth, who had Rasali's eyes and her effortless way of moving.

Valo started asking questions, first of the other workers and then of Kit. His boat-building experience meant the questions were good ones. Kit passed on the first things he had learned as a child on his father's sites and showed him the manipulation of the immense blocks and the tricky balance of material and plan, the strength of will that allows a man to direct a thousand people toward a single vision. Valo was too honest not to recognize Kit's mastery and too competitive not to try and meet Kit on his own ground. He came more often to visit the construction sites.

After a season, Kit took him aside. "You could be a builder if you wished."

Valo flushed. "Build things? You mean bridges?"

"Or houses or granges or retaining walls. Or bridges. You could make people's lives better."

"Change people's lives?" He frowned suddenly. "No."

"Our lives change all the time whether we want them to or not," Kit said. "Valo Ferry of Farside, you are intelligent. You are good with people. You learn quickly. If you were interested, I could start teaching you myself or send you to Atyar to study there."

"Valo Builder..." he said, trying it out, then: "No." But after that, whenever he had time free from ferrying or building boats, he was always to be found on the site. Kit knew that the answer would be different the next time he asked. There was for everything a possibility, an invisible pattern that could be made manifest given work and the right materials. Kit wrote to an old friend or two, finding contacts that would help Valo when the time came. He would not be ashamed of this new protegé.

The pillars and anchorages grew. Winter came and summer, and a second winter. There were falls, a broken arm, two sets of cracked ribs. Someone on Farside had her toes crushed when one of the stones slipped from its rollers and she lost the foot. The bridge was on schedule even after the delay caused by the slow rock-breaking. There were no problems with payroll or the Department of Roads or Empire, and only minor, manageable issues with the occasionally disruptive representatives from Triple or the local governors.

Kit knew he was lucky.

The first death came during one of Valo's visits.

It was early in the second winter of the bridge, and Kit had been in Farside for three months. He had already learned that winter meant gray skies and rain and sometimes snow. Soon they would have to stop the heavy work for the season. Still, it had been a good day and the workers had lifted and placed most of a course of stones.

Valo had returned after three weeks at Nearside building a boat for Jenna Bluefish. Kit found him staring up at the slim tower through a rain so faint it felt like fog. Halfway up the pillar, the black opening of the roadway arch looked out of place.

Valo said, "You're a lot farther along since I was here last. How tall now?"

Kit got this question a lot. "A hundred and five feet, more or less. A little over a quarter finished."

Valo smiled, shook his head. "Hard to believe it'll stay up."

"There's a tower in Atyar, black basalt and iron, five hundred feet. Five times this tall."

"It just looks so delicate," Valo said. "I know what you said, that most of the stress on the pillar is compression, but it still looks as though it'll snap in half."

"After a while you'll have more experience with suspension bridges and it will seem less…unsettling. Would you like to see the progress?"

Valo's eyes brightened. "May I? I don't want to get in the way."

"I haven't been up yet today and they'll be finishing up soon. Scaffold or stairwell?"

Valo looked at the scaffolding against one face of the pillar, the ladders tied into place within it, and shivered. "I can't believe people go up that. Stairs."

Kit followed Valo. The steep internal stair was three feet wide and endlessly turning, five steps up and then a platform, turn to the left and then five more steps and turn. Eventually the stairs would be lit by lanterns set into alcoves at every third turning, but today Kit and Valo felt their way up, fingers trailing along the cold damp stone, a small lantern in Valo's hand. The stairwell smelled of water and earth and the thin smell of the burning lamp oil. Some of the workers hated the stairs and preferred the ladders outside, but Kit liked it here. For these few moments he was part of his bridge, a strong bone buried deep in flesh he had created.

They came out at the top and paused a moment to look around the unfinished course, and at the black silhouette of the crane against the dulling sky. The last few workers were breaking down a shear-leg that had been used to move blocks. A lantern hung from a pole jammed into one of the holes the laborers would fill with rods and molten iron. Kit nodded to them as Valo went to an edge to look down.

"It is wonderful," Valo said, smiling. "Being high like this—you can look right down into people's kitchen yards. Look, Teli Carpenter has a pig smoking."

"You don't need to see it to know that," Kit said dryly. "I've been smelling it for two days."

Valo snorted. "Can you see as far as White Peak yet?"

"On a clear day, yes," Kit said. "I was up here two—"

A heavy sliding sound and a scream. Kit whirled to see one of the workers on her back, one of the shear-leg's timbers across her chest. Loreh Tanner, a local. Kit ran the few steps to Loreh and dropped beside her. One man, the man who had been working with her, said, "It slipped—oh, Loreh, please hang on," but Kit could see already that it was futile. She was pinned against the pillar, chest flattened, one shoulder visibly dislocated, unconscious, breathing labored. Foam bloomed from her lips, black in the lantern's bad light.

Kit took her cold hand. "It's all right, Loreh. It's all right." It was a lie and in any case she could not hear him, but the others would. "Get Hall," one of the workers said and Kit nodded: Hall was a surgeon. And then, "And get Obal, someone. Get her husband." Footsteps ran down the stairs and were lost into the hiss of rain just beginning and someone's crying and Loreh's wet breathing.

Kit glanced up. His chest heaving, Valo stood staring. Kit said to him, "Help find Hall," and when the boy did not move he repeated it, his voice sharper. Valo said nothing, did not stop looking at Loreh until he spun and ran down the stairs. Kit heard shouting far below as the first messenger ran toward the town.

Loreh took a last shuddering breath and died.

Kit looked at the others around Loreh's body. The man holding Loreh's other hand pressed his face against it crying helplessly. The two other workers left here knelt at her feet, a man and a woman, huddled close though they were not a couple. "Tell me," he said.

"I tried to stop it from hitting her," the woman said. She cradled one arm: obviously broken though she did not seem to have noticed. "But it just kept falling."

"She was tired. She must have gotten careless," the man said, and the broken-armed woman said, "I don't want to think about that sound."

Words fell from them like blood from a cut. This was what they needed right now, to speak and to be heard. So he listened, and when the others came, Loreh's husband Obal, white-lipped and angry-eyed, the surgeon Hall, and six other workers, Kit listened to them as well, and gradually moved them down through the pillar and back toward the warm lights and comfort of Farside.

Kit had lost people before and it was always like this. There would be tears tonight, and anger at him and at his bridge, anger at fate for permitting this. There would be sadness and nightmares. And there would be lovemaking and the holding close of children and friends and dogs—affirmations of life in the cold wet night.

His tutor at University had said, during one of her frequent digressions from materials and the principles of architecture, "Things will go wrong."

It was winter, but in spite of the falling snow they walked slowly to the coffee house, as Skossa looked for purchase for her cane. She continued, "On long projects, you'll forget that you're not one of them. But if there's an accident? You're slapped in the face with it. Whatever you're feeling? Doesn't matter. Guilty, grieving, alone, worried about the schedule. None of it. What matters is *their* feelings. So listen to them. Respect what they're going through."

She paused then, tapped her cane against the ground thoughtfully. "No, I lie. It does matter but you will have to find your own strength, your own resources elsewhere."

"Friends?" Kit said doubtfully. He knew already that he wanted a career like his father's. He would not be in the same place for more than a few years at a time.

"Yes, friends." Snow collected on Skossa's hair but she didn't seem to notice. "Kit, I worry about you. You're good with people, I've seen it. You like them. But there's a limit for you." He opened his mouth to protest but she held up her hand to silence him. "I know. You do care. But inside the framework of a project. Right now it's your studies. Later it'll be roads and bridges. But people around you—their lives go on outside the framework. They're not just tools to your hand, even likable tools. Your life should go on, too. You should have more than roads to live for. Because if something does go wrong, you'll need what *you're* feeling to matter, to someone somewhere, anyway."

Kit walked through Farside toward The Bitch. Most people were home or in one of the taverns by now, a village turned inward; but he heard footsteps running behind him. He turned quickly. It was not unknown for people reeling from a loss to strike at whatever they blamed, and sometimes it was a person.

It was Valo. Though his fists were balled, Kit could tell immediately that he was angry but that he was not looking for a fight. For a moment Kit wished he didn't need to listen, that he could just go back to his rooms and sleep for a thousand hours, but there was a stricken look in Valo's eyes: Valo, who looked so much like Rasali. He hoped that Rasali and Loreh hadn't been close.

Kit said gently, "Why aren't you inside? It's cold." As he said it, he realized suddenly that it *was* cold. The rain had settled into a steady cold flood.

"I will. I was, I mean, but I came out because I thought maybe I could find you, because—" The boy was shivering.

"Where are your friends? Let's get you inside. It'll be better there."

"No," he said. "I have to know first. It's like this always? If I do this, build things, it'll happen for me? Someone will die?"

"It might. It probably will, eventually."

Valo said an unexpected thing: "I see. It's just that she had just gotten married."

The blood on Loreh's lips, the wet sound of her crushed chest as she took her last breaths— "Yes," Kit said. "She had."

"I just…I had to know if I need to ready for this. I guess I'll find out."

"I hope you don't have to." The rain was getting heavier. "You should be inside, Valo."

Valo nodded. "Rasali—I wish she were here. She could help maybe. You should go in too. You're shivering."

Kit watched him go. Valo had not invited him to accompany him back into the light and the warmth. He knew better than to expect that, but for a moment he had permitted himself to hope otherwise.

Kit slipped through the stables and through the back door at The Bitch. Widson Innkeep, hands full of mugs for the taproom, saw him and nodded, face unsmiling but not hostile. That was good, Kit thought, as good as it would get tonight.

He entered his room and shut the door, leaned his back to it as if to hold the world out. Someone had already been in his room. A lamp had been lit against the darkness, a fire laid, and bread and cheese and a tankard of ale set by the window to stay cool. He began to cry.

The news went across the river by signal flags. No one worked on the bridge the next day or the day after that. Kit did all the right things, letting his grief and guilt overwhelm him only when he was alone, huddled in front of the fire in his room.

The third day, Rasali arrived from Nearside with a boat filled with crates of northland herbs on their way east. Kit was sitting in The Bitch's taproom, listening. People were coping, starting to look forward again. They should be able to get back to it soon, the next clear day. He would offer them something that would be an immediate, visible accomplishment, something different, perhaps guidelining the ramp.

He didn't see Rasali come into the taproom, only felt her hand on his shoulder and heard her voice in his ear. "Come with me," she murmured.

He looked up puzzled, as though she were a stranger. "Rasali Ferry, why are you here?"

She said only, "Come for a walk, Kit."

It was raining but he accompanied her anyway, pulling a scarf over his head when the first cold drops hit his face.

She said nothing as they splashed through Farside. She was leading him someplace but he didn't care where, grateful not to have to be the decisive one, the strong one. After a time she opened a door and led him through it into a small room filled with light and warmth.

"My house," she said. "And Valo's. He's still at the boatyard. Sit."

She pointed and Kit dropped onto the settle beside the fire. Rasali swiveled a pot hanging from a bracket out of the fire and ladled something into a mug. She handed it to him and sat. "So. Drink."

It was spiced porter and the warmth eased the tightness in his chest. "Thank you."

"Talk."

"This is such a loss for you all, I know," he said. "Did you know Loreh well?"

She shook her head. "This is not for me, this is for you. Tell me."

"I'm fine," he said, and when she didn't say anything, he repeated with a flicker of anger: "I'm *fine,* Rasali. I can handle this."

"Probably you can," Rasali said. "But you're not fine. She died and it was your bridge she died for. You don't feel responsible? I don't believe it."

"Of course I feel responsible," he snapped.

The fire cast gold light across her broad cheekbones when she turned her face to him, but she said nothing, only looked at him and waited.

"She's not the first," Kit said, surprising himself. "The first project I had sole charge of, a toll gate. Such a little project, such a silly little project to lose someone on. The wood frame for the passageway collapsed before we got the keystone in. The whole arch came down. Someone got killed." It had been a very young man, slim and tall with a limp. He was raising his little sister. She hadn't been more than ten. Running loose in the fields around the site, she had missed the collapse, the boy's death. Dafuen? Naus? He couldn't remember his name. And the girl—what had her name been? *I should remember. I owe that much to them.*

"Every time I lose someone," he said at last, "I remember the others. There've been twelve in seventeen years. Not so many, considering. Building's dangerous. My record's better than most."

"But it doesn't matter, does it?" she said. "You still feel you killed each one of them, as surely as if you'd thrown them off a bridge yourself."

"It's my responsibility. The first one, Duar—" *that* had been his name; there it was. The name loosened something in Kit. His face warmed: tears, hot tears running down his face.

"It's all right," she said. She held him until he stopped crying.

"How did you know?" he said finally.

"I am the eldest surviving member of the Ferry family," she said. "My father died. My mother. My aunt died seven years ago. And then I watched my brother leave to cross the mist, three years ago now. It was a perfect day, calm and sunny, but he never made it. He went instead of me because the river felt wrong to me that day. It could have been me. It should have, maybe. So I understand."

She stretched a little. "Not that most people don't. If Petro Housewright sends his daughter to select timber in the mountains and she doesn't come back—eaten by wolves, struck by lightning, I don't know—is Petro to blame? It's probably the wolves or the lightning. Maybe it's the daughter, if she did something stupid. And it *is* Petro, a little; she wouldn't have been there at all if he hadn't sent her. And it's her mother for being fearless and teaching that to her daughter, and Thom Green for wanting a new room to his house. Everyone except maybe the wolves feels responsible. This path leads nowhere. Loreh would have died sooner or later." Rasali added softly, "We all do."

"Can you accept death so readily?" he asked. "Yours even?"

She leaned back, her face suddenly weary. "What else can I do, Kit? Someone must ferry and I am better suited than most—and by more than my blood. I love the mist, its currents and the smell of it and the power in my body as I push us all through. Petro's daughter Cilar—she did not want to die when the wolves came, I'm sure, but she loved selecting timber."

"If it comes for you?" he said. "Would you be so sanguine then?"

She laughed and the pensiveness was gone. "No indeed. I will curse the stars and go down fighting. But it will still have been a wonderful thing, to cross the mist."

At University, Kit's relationships had all been casual. There were lectures that everyone attended, and he lived near streets and pubs crowded with students; but the physical students had a tradition of keeping to themselves that was rooted in the personal preferences of their predecessors and in their own. The only people who worked harder than the engineers were the ale-makers, the University joke went. Kit and the other physical students talked and drank and roomed and slept together.

In his third year, he met Domhu Canna at the arcade where he bought vellums and paper: a small woman with a heart-shaped face and hair in black clouds that she kept somewhat confined by gray ribbons. She was a philosophical student from a city two thousand miles to the east, on the coast.

He was fascinated. Her mind was abrupt and fish-quick and made connections he didn't understand. To her, everything was a metaphor, a symbol for something else. People, she said, could be better understood by comparing their lives to animals, to the seasons, to the structure of certain lyrical poems, to a gambling game.

This was another form of pattern-making, he saw. Perhaps people were like teamed oxen to be led, or like metals to be smelted and shaped to one's purpose, or like the stones for a dry-laid wall, which had to be carefully selected for shape and strength, sorted, and placed. This last suited him best. What held them together was not external mortar but their own weight and the planning and patience of the drystone builder. But it was an inadequate metaphor. People were this, but they were all the other things as well.

He never understood what Domhu found attractive in him. They never talked about regularizing their relationship. When her studies were done halfway through his final year, she returned to her city to help found a new university, and in any case her people did not enter into term marriages. They separated amicably and with a sense of loss on his part at least, but it did not occur to him until years later that things might have been different.

The winter was rainy but there were days they could work and they did. By spring, there had been other deaths unrelated to the bridge on both banks: a woman who died in childbirth, a child who had never breathed properly in his short life, two fishers lost when they capsized, several who died for the various reasons that old or sick people died.

Over the spring and summer they finished the anchorages, featureless masses of blocks and mortar anchored to the bedrock. They were buried so that only a few courses of stone showed above the ground. The anchoring bolts were each tall as a man, hidden behind the portals through which the chains would pass.

The Farside pillar was finished by midwinter of the third year, well before the Nearside tower. Jenner and Teniant Planner had perfected a signal system that allowed detailed technical information to pass between the banks, and Kit took full advantage of it. Documents traveled each time a ferry crossed. Rasali made thirty-eight trips. Though he spent much of his time with Kit, Valo made nineteen. Kit did not cross the mist at all unless the flags told him he must.

It was early spring and Kit was in Farside when the signals went up: *Message. Imperial seal.* He went to Rasali at once.

"I can't go," she said. "I just got here yesterday. The Big Ones—"

"I have to get across and Valo's at Nearside. There's news from the capital."

"News has always waited before."

"No it hasn't. News waited restlessly, pacing along the levee until we could pick it up."

"Use the flags," she said impatiently.

"The seals can't be broken by anyone but me or Jenner. He's over here. I'm sorry," he said, thinking of her brother, dead four years before.

"If you die no one can read it," she said, but they left just after dusk anyway. "If we must go, better then than earlier or later."

He met her at the upper dock at dusk. The sky was streaked with bright bands of green and gold, clouds catching the last of the sun so that they glowed but radiated no light. The current down the river was steady. The mist between the levees was already in shadow, smooth dunes twenty feet high.

Rasali waited silently, coiling and uncoiling a rope in her hands. Beside her stood two women, a man, and a dog: dealers in spices returning from the plantations of Gloth, the dog whining and restless. Kit was burdened with document cases filled with vellum and paper rolled tightly and wrapped in oilcloth. Rasali seated the merchants and their dog in the ferry's bow, their forty crates of cinnamon and nutmeg amidships, Kit in the back near her. In silence she untied and pushed away from the dock.

She stood at the stern, braced against the scull. For a moment he could pretend that this was water they moved on and he half expected to hear sloshing, but the big paddle made no noise. It was so quiet that he could hear her breath, the dog's nervous panting in front, and his own pulse, too fast. Then the *Crossing* slid up the long smooth slope of a dune and there was no possibility that this could be anything but mist.

He heard a soft sighing, like air entering a once-sealed room. It was hard to see so far, but the lingering light showed him mist heaving on the face of a neighboring dune, like a bubble coming to the surface of mud. The dome grew and then burst. There was a gasp from one of the women. A shape rolled away, too dark for Kit to see more than its length.

"What—" he said in wonder.

"Fish," Rasali breathed to Kit. "Not small ones. They are biting tonight. We should not have come."

It was night now. The first tiny moon appeared, followed by stars. Rasali oared gently through the dunes, face turned to the sky. At first he thought she was praying but she was navigating. There were more fish now: each time the sighing sound, the dark shape half seen. He heard someone singing, the voice carrying somehow, from far behind.

"The fishers," Rasali said. "They will stay close to the levees tonight. I wish...."

But she left the wish unspoken. They were over the deep mist now. He could not say how he knew this. He had a sudden vision of the bridge overhead, a black span bisecting the star-spun sky, the parabolic arch of the chains perhaps visible, perhaps not. People would stride across the river an arrow's flight overhead, unaware of this place beneath. Perhaps they would stop and look over the bridge's railings but they would be too high to see the fish as any but small shadows—supposing they saw them at all, supposing they stopped at all. The Big Ones would be novelties, weird creatures that caused a safe shiver, like hearing a frightening story late at night.

Perhaps Rasali saw the same thing for she said suddenly, "Your bridge. It will change all this."

"It must. I am sorry," he said again. "We are not meant to be here on mist."

"We are not meant to cross this without passing through it. Kit—" Rasali said as though starting a sentence and then fell silent. After a moment she began to speak again, her voice low, as though she were speaking to herself. "The soul often hangs in a balance of some sort. Tonight do I lie down in the high fields with Dirna Tanner or not? At the fair, do I buy ribbons or wine? For the new ferry's headboard, do I use camphor or pearwood? Small things. A kiss, a ribbon, a grain that coaxes the knife this way or that. They are not, Kit Meinem of Atyar. Our souls wait for our answer because any answer changes us. This is why I wait to decide what I feel about your bridge. I'm waiting until I know how I will be changed."

"You never know how things will change you," Kit said.

"If you do not, you have not waited to find out." There was a popping noise barely a stone's throw to starboard. "Quiet."

On they moved. In daylight, Kit knew, the trip took less than an hour but now it seemed much longer. Perhaps it was. He looked up at the stars and thought they had moved but perhaps not.

His teeth were clenched, as were all his muscles. When he tried to relax them, he realized it was not fear that cramped him but something else, something outside him. Rasali's stroke faltered.

He recognized it now, the sound that was not a sound, like the deepest pipes on an organ, a drone too low to hear but which turned his bones to liquid and his muscles to flaked and rusting iron. His breath labored from his chest in grunts. His vision narrowed. Moving as though through honey, he strained his hands to his head, cradling it. He could not see Rasali except as a gloom against the slightly less gloom of the mist but he heard her pant, tiny pain-filled breaths like an injured dog.

The thrumming in his body pounded at his bones now, dissolving them. He wanted to cry out but there was no air left in his lungs. He realized suddenly that the mist beneath them was raising itself. It piled up along the boat's sides. *I never got to finish the bridge*, he thought. *And I never kissed her.* Did Rasali have any regrets?

The mound roiled and became a hill, which became a mountain obscuring part of the sky. The crest melted into curls and there was a shape inside, large and dark as night itself, that slid and followed the collapsing mist. It seemed not to move, but he knew that was only because of the size of the thing, that it took ages for its full length to pass. That was all he saw before his eyes slipped shut.

How long he lay there in the bottom of the boat, he didn't know. At some point he realized he was there. Some time later he found he could move again, his bones and muscles back to what they should be. The dog was barking. "Rasali?" he said shakily. "Are we sinking?"

"Kit." Her voice was a thread. "You're still alive. I thought we were dead."

"That was a Big One?"

"I don't know. No one has ever seen one. Maybe it was just a Fairly Large One."

The old joke. Kit choked on a weak laugh.

"Shit," Rasali said in the darkness. "I dropped the oar."

"Now what?" he said.

"I have smaller spares, but it's going to take longer and we'll land in the wrong place. We'll have to tie off and then walk up to get help."

I'm alive, he did not say. *I can walk a thousand miles tonight.*

It was nearly dawn before they got to Nearside. The two big moons rose just before they landed, a mile south of the dock. The spice traders and their dog went on ahead while Kit and Rasali secured the boat and walked up together. Halfway home, Valo came down at a dead run.

"I was waiting and you didn't come—" He was pale and panting. "But they told me, the other passengers, that you made it and—"

"Valo." Rasali hugged him and held him hard. "We're safe, little one. We're here. It's done."

"I thought...." he said.

"I know," she said. "Valo, please, I am so tired. Can you get the *Crossing* up to the dock? I am going to my house and I will sleep for a day, and I don't care if the Empress herself is tapping her foot, it's going to wait." She released Valo, saluted Kit with a weary smile, and walked up the long flank of the levee. Kit watched her leave.

The "Imperial seal" was a letter from Atyar, some underling arrogating authority and asking for clarification on a set of numbers Kit had sent—scarcely worth the trip at any time, let alone across mist on a bad night. Kit cursed the capital, Empire, and the Department of Roads, and then sent the information along with a tautly worded paragraph about seals and their appropriate use.

Two days later, he got news that would have brought him across the mist in any case. The caravan carrying the first eyebars and bolts was twelve miles out on the Hoic Mine Road. Kit and his ironmaster Tandreve Smith rode out to meet the wagons as they crept southward and found them easing down a gradual slope near Oud village. The carts were long and built strong, their contents covered, each pulled by a team of tough-legged oxen with patient expressions. Their pace was slow and drivers walked beside them, singing something unfamiliar to Kit's city-bred ears.

"Ox-tunes. We used to sing these at my uncle's farm," Tandreve said, and sang:

> *"Remember last night's dream,*
> *the sweet cold grass, the lonely cows.*
> *You had your bollocks then."*

Tandreve chuckled, and Kit with her.

One of the drivers wandered over as Kit pulled his horse to a stop. Unattended, her team moved forward anyway. "Folks," she said and nodded. A taciturn woman.

Kit swung down from the saddle. "These are the chains?"

"You're from the bridge?"

"Kit Meinem of Atyar."

The woman nodded again. "Berallit Red-Ox of Ilver. Your smiths are sitting on the tail of the last wagon."

One of the smiths, a rangy man with singed eyebrows, loped forward to meet them and introduced himself as Jared Toss of Little Hoic. They walked beside the carts as they talked, and he threw aside a tarp to show Kit and Tandreve what they carried: stacks of iron eyebars, each a rod ten feet long with eyes at either end. Tandreve walked sideways as she inspected them. She and Jared soon lost themselves in a technical discussion. Kit kept them company, leading Tandreve's forgotten horse and his own, content for the moment to let the masters talk it out. He moved a little forward until he was abreast of the oxen. *Remember last night's dream,* he thought and then: *I wonder what Rasali dreamt?*

After that night on the mist, Rasali seemed to have no bad days. She took people the day after they arrived, no matter what the weather or the mist's character. The tavern keepers grumbled at this but the decrease in time each visitor stayed was made up for by the increase in numbers of serious-eyed men and women sent by firms in Atyar to establish offices in the towns on the River's far side. It made things easier for the bridge as well, since Kit and others could move back and forth as needed. Kit remained reluctant, more so since the near-miss.

There was enough business for two boats. Valo volunteered to ferry more often but Rasali refused the help, allowing him to ferry only when she couldn't prevent it. "The Big Ones don't seem to care about me this winter," she said to him, "but I can't say they would feel the same about tender meat like you." With Kit she was more honest. "If he is to leave ferrying to go study in the capital, it's best sooner than later. Mist will be dangerous until the last ferry crosses it. And even then, even after your bridge is done."

It was only Rasali who seemed to have this protection. The fishing people had as many problems as in any year. Denis Redboat lost his coracle when it was rammed ("—by a Medium-Large One," he laughed in the tavern later: sometimes the oldest jokes really were the best), though he was fished out by a nearby boat before he sank too deep. The rash was only superficial but his hair grew back only in patches.

Kit sat in the crowded beer garden of The Deer's Hart watching Rasali and Valo cover with fishskin a little pinewood skiff in the boat yard next door. Valo had called out a greeting when Kit first sat down and Rasali turned her head to smile at him, but after that they ignored him. Some of the locals stopped by to greet him and the barman stayed for some time, telling him about the ominous yet unchanging ache in his back, but for most of the afternoon Kit was alone in the sun, drinking cellar-cool porter and watching the boat take shape.

In the midsummer of the fourth year, it was rare for Kit to have all the afternoon of a beautiful day to himself. The anchorages had been finished for some months. So had the rubble-filled ramps that led to the arched passages through each pillar. The pillars themselves had taken longer, and the granite saddles that would support the chains over the towers had only just been put in place.

They were only slightly behind on Kit's deadlines for most of the materials. More than a thousand of the eyebars and bolts for the chains were laid out in rows, the iron smelling of the linseed oil used to protect them during transit. More were expected in before winter. Close to the ramps were the many fishskin ropes and cables that would be needed to bring the first chain across the gap. They were irreplaceable—probably the most valuable thing on the work sites—and were treated accordingly, kept in closed tents that reeked.

Kit's high-work specialists were here, too: the men and women who would do the first perilous tasks, mostly experts who had worked on other big spans or the towers of Atyar.

Valo and Rasali were not alone in the boat yard. Rasali had sent to the ferry folk of Ubmie a hundred miles to the south, and they had arrived a few days before: a woman and her cousin, Chell and Lan Crosser. The strangers had the same massive shoulders and good looks the Ferrys had, but they shared a faraway expression of their own. The river was broader at Ubmie, deeper, so perhaps death was closer to them. Kit wondered what they thought of his task. The bridge would cut into ferry trade for many hundreds of miles on either side and Ubmie had been reviewed as a possible site for the bridge, but they must not have resented it or they would not be here.

Everything waited on the ferry folk. The next major task was to bring the lines across the river to connect the piers—fabricating the chains required temporary cables and catwalks be in place first—but this could not be rushed. Rasali, Valo, and the Crossers all needed to feel at the same time that it was safe to cross. Kit tried not to be impatient. In any case he had plenty to do—items to add to lists, formal reports and polite updates to send to the many interested parties in Atyar and Triple, instructions to pass on to the ropemakers, the masons, the road-builders, the exchequer. And Jenner: Kit had written to the capital, and the Department of Roads was offering Jenner the lead on the second bridge across the river, to be built a few hundred miles to the north. Kit was to deliver the cartel the next time they were on the same side, but he was grateful the officials had agreed to leave Jenner with him until the first chain on this bridge was in place. Things to do.

He pushed all this from his mind. *Later,* he said to the things, half-apologetically. *I'll deal with you later. For now just let me sit in the sun and watch other people work.*

The sun slanted peach-gold through the oak's leaves before Rasali and Valo finished for the day. The skiff was finished, an elegant tiny curve of pale wood, red-dyed fishskin, and fading sunlight. Kit leaned against the fence as they tossed a cup of water over its bow and then drew it into the shadows of the storage shed. Valo took off at a run—*so much energy, even after a long day;* ah, youth—as Rasali walked to the fence and leaned on it from her side.

"It's beautiful," he said.

She rolled her neck. "I know. We make good boats. Are you hungry? Your busy afternoon must have raised an appetite."

He had to laugh. "We laid the capstone this morning. I *am* hungry."

"Come on then. Thalla will feed us all."

Dinner was simple. The Deer's Hart was better known for its beer than its foods, but the stew Thalla served was savory with chervil and thick enough to stand a spoon in. Valo had friends to be with, so they ate with Chell and Lan, who turned out to be like Rasali, calm but light-hearted. At dusk, the Crossers left to explore the Nearside taverns, leaving Kit and Rasali to watch heat lightning in the west. The air was thick and warm, soft as wool.

"You never come up to the work sites on either side," Kit said suddenly after a comfortable, slightly drunken silence. He inspected his earthenware mug, empty now except for the smell of yeast.

Rasali had given up on the benches and sat instead on one of the garden tables. She leaned back until she lay supine, face toward the sky. "I've been busy, perhaps you noticed?"

"It's more than that. Everyone finds time here and there. And you used to."

"I did, didn't I? I just haven't seen the point lately. The bridge changes everything but I don't see yet how it changes me. So I wait until it's time. Perhaps it's like the mist."

"What about now?"

She rolled her head until her cheek lay against the rough wood of the tabletop: looking at him, he could tell, though her eyes were hidden in shadows. What did she see, he wondered. What was she hoping to see? It pleased him but made him nervous.

"Come to the tower now, tonight," he said. "Soon everything changes. We pull the ropes across and make the chains and hang the supports and lay the road. It stops being a project and becomes a bridge, a road. But tonight it's still just two towers and some plans. Rasali, climb it with me. I can't describe what it's like up there—the wind, the sky all around you, the river below." He flushed at the urgency in his voice. When she remained silent he added, "You change whether you wait for it or not."

"There's lightning," she said.

"It runs from cloud to cloud," he said. "Not to earth."

"Heat lightning." She sat up. "So show me this place."

The work site was abandoned. The sky overhead had filled with clouds lit from within by the lightning, which was worse than no light at all since it ruined their night vision. They staggered across the site, trying to plan their paths in the moments of light, doggedly moving through the darkness. "Shit," Rasali said suddenly in the darkness, then: "Tripped over something or other. Ghost sheep." Kit found himself laughing.

They took the internal stairs instead of the scaffold. Kit knew them thoroughly, knew every irregular turn and riser, so he counted them aloud to Rasali as he led her by the hand. They reached one hundred and ninety-four before they saw light from a flash of lightning overhead, two hundred and eighteen when they finally stepped onto the roof, panting for air.

They were not alone. A woman gasped; she and the man with her bolted down the stairs, laughing. Rasali said with satisfaction, "Sera Oakfield. I'd recognize that laugh anywhere. Then that was Erno Bridgeman with her."

"He took his name from the bridge?" Kit asked but Rasali said only, "Oh," in a child's voice. Silent lightning painted the sky over her head in sudden strokes of purple-white, shot through what seemed a dozen layers of cloud, an incomprehensible complexity of light and shadow.

"The sky is so much closer." She walked to the edge and looked down at Nearside. Dull gold light poured from doors open to the heavy air. Kit stayed where he was, content to watch her. The light—when there was light—was shadowless and her face looked young and full of wonder. After a time she came to him.

They said nothing, only kissed and then made love in a nest of their discarded clothes. Kit felt the stone of his bridge against his knees, his back. It was still warm as skin from the day's heat, but not as warm as Rasali. She was softer than the rocks and tasted sweet.

A feeling he could not have described cracked open his chest, his throat, his belly. It had been a long time since he had had sex, not met his own needs. He had nearly forgotten the delight of it, the sharp rising shock of his coming, the rocking ocean of hers. Even their awkwardness pleased him, because it held in it the possibility of doing this again, and better.

When they were done they talked. "You know my goal, to build this bridge." Kit looked down at her face, there and gone in the flickering of the lightning. "But I do not know yours."

Rasali laughed softly. "Yet you have seen me succeed a thousand times, and fail a few. I wish to live well."

"That's not a goal," Kit said.

"Why? Because it's not yours? Which is better, Kit Meinem of Atyar? A single great victory or a thousand small ones?" And then: "Tomorrow," Rasali said. "We will take the rope across tomorrow."

"You're sure?" Kit asked.

"That's a strange statement coming from you. The bridge is all about crossing being a certainty, yes? Like the sun coming up each morning? We agreed this afternoon. It's time."

Dawn came early with the innkeeper's rap on the door. Kit woke disoriented, tangled in the sheets of his little cupboard bed. After he and Rasali had come down from the pillar, Rasali to sleep and Kit to do everything that needed to happen before the rope was brought across, all in the few hours remaining to the night. His skin smelled of Rasali but he was stunned with lack of sleep, and had trouble believing the sex had been real. But there was stone dust ground into his palms. He smiled and, though it was high summer, sang a spring song from Atyar as he quickly washed and dressed. He drank a bowl filled with broth in the taproom. It was tangy, lukewarm. A single small perch stared up at him from a salted eye. Kit left the fish, and left the inn.

The clouds and the lightning were gone. Early as it was the sky was already pale and hot. The news was everywhere and the entire town, or so it seemed, drifted with Kit to the work site, flowed over the levee, and settled onto the bank.

The river was a blinding creamy ribbon, looking as it had the first time he had seen it; and for a minute he felt dislocated in time. High mist was seen as a good omen and though he did not believe in omens he was nevertheless glad. The signal towers' flags hung limp against the hot blue-white sky.

Kit walked down to Rasali's boat, nearly hidden in its own tight circle of people. As Kit approached, Valo called, "Hey, Kit!" Rasali looked up. Her smile was like welcome shade on a bright day. The circle opened to accept him.

"Greetings, Valo Ferry of Farside, Rasali Ferry of Farside," he said. When he was close enough, he clasped Rasali's hands in his own, loving their warmth despite the day's heat.

"Kit." She kissed his mouth to a handful of muffled hoots and cheers from the bystanders and a surprised noise from Valo. She tasted like chicory.

Daell Cabler nodded absently to Kit. She was the lead ropemaker. She, her husband Stivvan, and the journeymen and masters they had summoned were inspecting the hundreds of fathoms of twisted fishskin cord, loading them without kinks onto spools three feet across and loading those onto a wooden frame bolted to *The Tranquil Crossing*.

The rope was thin, not much more than a cord, narrower than Kit's smallest finger. It looked fragile, and nothing like strong enough to carry its own weight for a quarter of a mile. The tests said otherwise.

Several of the stronger people from the bridge handed down small heavy crates to Valo and Chell Crosser, in the bow. Silverwork from Hedeclin and copper in bricks: the ferry was to be weighted somewhat forward, which would make the first part of the crossing more difficult but should help by the end, as the cord paid out and took on weight from the mist.

"—We think, anyway," Valo had said, two months back when he and Rasali had discussed the plan with Kit. "But we don't know. No one's done this before." Kit had nodded and not for the first time wished that the river had been a little less broad. Upriver perhaps—but no, this had been the only option. He did write to an old classmate back in Atyar, a man who now taught the calculus, and presented their solution. His friend had written back to say that it looked as though it ought to work, but that he knew little of mist.

One end of the rope snaked along the ground and up the levee. No one touched the rope. They crowded close but left a narrow lane and stepped only carefully across it. Daell and Stivvan Cabler followed the lane back up and over the levee, to check the temporary anchor at the Nearside pillar's base.

There was a wait. People sat on the grass or walked back to watch the Cablers. Someone brought broth and small beer from the fishers' tavern. Valo and Rasali and the two Crossers were remote, focused already on what came next.

And for himself? Kit was wound up but it wouldn't do to show anything but a calm, confident front. He walked among the watchers and exchanged words or a smile with each of them. He knew them all by now, even the children.

It was nearly midmorning before Daell and Stivvan returned. The ferryfolk took their positions in the *Crossing*, two to each side, far enough apart that they could pull on different rhythms. Kit was useless freight until they got to the other side, so he sat at the bow where his weight might do some good. Uni stumbled as she was helped into the boat's stern: she would monitor the rope but, as she told them all, she was nervous: she had never crossed the mist. "I think I'll wait 'til the catwalks go up before I return," she added. "Stivvan can sleep without me 'til then."

"Ready, Kit?" Rasali called forward.

"Yes," he said.

"Daell? Lan? Chell? Valo?" Assent all around.

"A historic moment," Valo announced. "The day the mist was bridged."

"Make yourself useful, boy," Rasali said. "Prepare to scull."

"Right," Valo said.

"Push us off," she said to the people on the dock. A cheer went up.

The dock and all the noises behind them disappeared almost immediately. The ferryfolk had been right that it was a good day for such an undertaking. The mist was a smooth series of ripples no taller than a man, and so dense that the *Crossing* rode high despite the extra weight and drag. It was the gentlest he had ever seen the river.

Kit's eyes ached from the brightness. "It will work?" Kit said, meaning the rope and their trip across the mist and the bridge itself—a question rather than a statement: unable to help himself, even though he had worked the calculations himself and had Jenner and Daell and Stivvan and Valo and a specialist in Atyar all check them, even though it was a child's question. Isolated in the mist, even competence seemed insufficient.

"Yes," Daell Cabler said from aft.

The rowers said little. At one point Rasali murmured into the deadened air, "To the right," and Valo and Lan Crosser changed their stroke to avoid a gentle mound a few feet high directly in their path. Mostly the *Crossing* slid steadily across the regular swells. Unlike his other trips, Kit saw no dark shapes in the mist, large or small. From here they could not see the dock, but the levee ahead was scattered with Farsiders waiting for the work they would do when the ferry landed.

There was nothing he could do to help, so Kit watched Rasali scull in the blazing sun. The work got harder as the rope spooled out until she and the others panted. Shining with sweat, her skin was nearly as bright as the mist in the sunlight, and he wondered how she could bear the light without burning. Her face looked solemn, intent on the eastern shore. Her eyes were alight with reflections from the mist. Then he recognized her expression. It was joy.

How will she bear it, he thought suddenly, *when there is no more ferrying to be done?* He had known that she loved what she did but he had never realized just how much. He felt as though he had been kicked in the gut. What would it do to her? His bridge would destroy this thing that she loved, that gave her name. How could he not have thought of that? "Rasali," he said, unable to stay silent.

"Not now," she said. The rowers panted as they dug in.

"It's like…pulling through dirt," Valo gasped.

"Quiet," Rasali snapped and then they were silent except for their laboring breath. Kit's own muscles knotted sympathetically. Foot by foot the ferry heaved forward. At some point they were close enough to the Farside upper dock that someone threw a rope to Kit and at last he could do something, however inadequate. He took the rope and pulled. The rowers pushed for their final strokes. The boat slid up beside the dock. People swarmed aboard, securing the boat to the dock, the rope to a temporary anchor on the bank.

Released, the Ferrys and the Crossers embraced, laughing a little dizzily. They walked up the levee toward Farside town and did not look back.

Kit left the ferry to join Jenner Ellar.

It was hard work. The rope's end had to be brought over an oiled stone saddle on the levee and down to a temporary anchor and capstan at the Farside pillar's base, a task that involved driving a team of oxen through a temporary gap Jenner had cut into the levee: a risk but one that had to be taken.

More oxen were harnessed to the capstan. Daell Cabler was still pale and shaking from the crossing, but after a glass of something cool and dark, she and her Farside counterparts walked the rope to look for any new weak spots. They found none. Jenner stayed with the capstan. Daell and Kit returned to the temporary saddle in the levee, the notch polished like glass and gleaming with oil.

The rope was released from the dockside anchor. The rope over the saddle whined as it took the load and flattened, and there was a deep pinging noise as it swung out to make a single line down from the saddle, down into the mist. The oxen at the capstan dug in.

The next hours were the tensest of Kit's life. For a time, the rope did not appear to change. The capstan moaned and clicked, and at last the rope slid by inches, by feet, through the saddle. He could do nothing but watch and rework all the calculations yet again in his mind. He did not see Rasali, but Valo came up after a time to watch the progress. Answering his questions settled Kit's nerves. The calculations were correct. He had done this before. He was suddenly starved and voraciously ate the food that Valo had brought for him. How long had it been since the broth at

The Fish? Hours. Most of a day.

The oxen puffed and grunted and were replaced with new teams. Even lubricated and with leather sleeves, the rope moved reluctantly across the saddle, but it did move. And then the pressure started to ease and the rope paid through the saddle faster. The sun was westering when at last the rope lifted free of the mist. By dusk, the rope was sixty feet above it, stretched humming-tight between the Farside and Nearside levees and the temporary anchors.

Just before dark, Kit saw the flags go up on the signal tower: *secure*.

Kit worked on and then seconded projects for five years after he left University. His father knew men and women at the higher levels in the Department of Roads, and his old tutor, Skossa Timt, knew more, so many were high-profile works, but he loved all of them, even his first lead, the little toll gate where the boy, Duar, had died.

All public work—drainage schemes, roadwork, amphitheaters, public squares, sewers, alleys and mews—was alchemy. It took the invisible patterns that people made as they lived, and turned them into stone and brick and wood and space. Kit built things that moved people through the intangible architecture that was his mind and his notion—and Empire's notion—of how their lives could be better.

The first major project he led was a replacement for a collapsed bridge in the Four Peaks region north of Atyar. The original had been a chain suspension bridge but much smaller than the mist bridge would be, crossing only a hundred yards, its pillars only forty feet high. With maintenance, it had survived heavy use for three centuries, shuddering under the carts that brought quicksilver ore down to the smelting village of Oncalion; but after the heavy snowfalls of what was subsequently called the Wolf Winter, one of the gorge's walls collapsed, taking the north pillar with it and leaving nowhere stable to rebuild. It was easier to start over, two hundred yards upstream.

The people of Oncalion were not genial. Hard work made for hard men and women. There was a grim, desperate edge to their willingness to labor on the bridge, because their livelihood and their lives were dependent on the mine. They had to be stopped at the end of each day or, dangerous as it was, they would work through moonlit nights.

But it was lonely work, even for Kit who did not mind solitude, and when the snows of the first winter brought a halt to construction, he returned with some relief to Atyar to stay with his father. Davell Meinem was old now. His memory was weakening though still strong enough. He spent his days overseeing construction of a vast and fabulous public maze of dry-laid stones brought from all over Empire: his final project, he said to Kit, an accurate prophecy. Skossa Timt had died during the Wolf Winter, but many of Kit's classmates were still in the capital. Kit spent evenings with them, attended lectures and concerts, entered for the season into a casual relationship with an architect who specialized in waterworks.

Kit returned to the site at Oncalion as soon as the roads cleared. In his absence, through the snows and melt-off, the people of Oncalion had continued to work in the bitter cold, laying course after course of stone. The work had to be redone.

The second summer, they worked every day and moonlit nights and Kit worked beside them.

Kit counted the bridge as a failure although it was coming in barely over budget and only a couple of months late, and no one had died. It was an ugly design; the people of Oncalion had worked hard but joylessly; and there was all his dissatisfaction and guilt about the work that had to be done anew.

Perhaps there was something in the tone of his letters to his father, for there came a day in early autumn that Davell Meinem arrived in Oncalion, riding a sturdy mountain horse and accompanied by a journeyman who vanished immediately into one of the village's three taverns. It was the middle of the afternoon.

"I want to see this bridge of yours," Davell said. He looked weary but straight-backed as ever. "Show it to me."

"We'll go tomorrow," Kit said. "You must be tired."

"Now," Davell said.

They walked up from the village together. It was a cool day and bright, though the road was overshadowed with pines and fir trees. Basalt outcroppings were stained dark green and black with lichens. His father moved slowly, pausing often for breath. They met a steady trickle of local people leading heavy-laden ponies. The roadbed across the bridge wasn't quite complete and could not take carts yet, but ponies could cross carrying ore in baskets. Oncalion was already smelting these first small loads.

At the bridge, Davell asked the same questions he had asked when Kit was a child playing on his work sites. Kit found himself responding as he had so many years before, eager to explain—or excuse—each decision; and always, always the ponies passing.

They walked down to the older site. The pillar had been gutted for stones so all that was left was rubble, but it gave them a good view of the new bridge: the boxy pillars, the curve of the main chains, the thick vertical suspender chains, the slight sprung arch of the bulky roadbed. It looked as clumsy as a suspension bridge could. Yet another pony crossed, led by a woman singing something in the local dialect.

"It's a good bridge," Davell said.

Kit shook his head. His father, who had been known for his sharp tongue on the work sites though never to his son, said, "A bridge is a means to an end. It only matters because of what it does. Leads from *here* to *there*. If you do your work right they won't notice it, any more than you notice where quicksilver comes from, most times. It's a good bridge because they are already using it. Stop feeling sorry for yourself, Kit."

It was a big party that night. The Farsiders (and, Kit knew, the Nearsiders) drank and danced under the shadow of their bridge-to-be. Torchlight and firelight touched the stones of the tower base and anchorage, giving them mass and meaning, but above their light the tower was a black outline, the absence of stars. Torches ringed the tower's parapet; they seemed no more than gold stars among the colder ones.

Kit walked among them. Everyone smiled or waved and offered to stand him drinks but no one spoke much with him. It was as though the lifting of the cable had separated him from them. The immense towers had not done this; he had still been one of them to some degree at least—the instigator of great labors but still, one of them. But now, for tonight anyway, he was the man who bridged the mist. He had not felt so lonely since his first day here. Even Loreh Tanner's death had not severed him so completely from their world.

On every project, there was a day like this. It was possible that the distance came from him, he realized suddenly. He came to a place and built something, passing through the lives of people for a few months or years. And then he left. A road through dangerous terrain or a bridge across mist saved lives and increased trade, but it changed the world as well. It was his job to make a thing and then leave to make the next one—but it was also his preference, not to remain and see what he had done. What would Nearside and Farside look like in ten years, in fifty? He had never returned to a previous site.

It was harder this time or perhaps just different. Perhaps *he* was different. He was staying longer this time because of the size of the project, and he had allowed himself to love the country on either side of the bridge. To have more was to have more to miss when he eventually left.

Rasali—what would her life look like?

Valo danced by, his arm around a woman half a head taller than he—Rica Bridger—and Kit caught his arm. "Where is Rasali?" he shouted, then knowing he could not be heard over the noise of drums and pipes, he mouthed *Rasali*. He didn't hear what Valo said but followed his pointing hand.

Rasali was alone, flat on her back on the river side of the levee, looking up. There were no moons, so the Sky Mist hung close overhead, a river of stars that poured east to west. Kit knelt a few feet away. "Rasali Ferry of Farside."

Her teeth flashed in the dark. "Kit Meinem of Atyar."

He lay beside her. The grass was like bad straw, coarse against his back and neck. Without looking at him she passed a jar of something. Its taste was strong as tar and Kit gasped for a moment.

"I did not mean…." he started but trailed off, unsure how to continue.

"Yes," she said and he knew she had heard the words he didn't say. Her voice contained a shrug. "Many people born into a Ferry family never cross the mist."

"But you—" He stopped, felt carefully for his words. "Maybe others don't but you do. And I think maybe you must do so."

"Just as you must build," she said softly. "That's clever of you to realize that."

"And there will be no need after this, will there? Not on boats anyway. We'll still need fishskin, so the fishers will still go out, but they—"

"—stay close to shore," she said.

"And you?" he asked.

"I don't know, Kit. Days come, days go. I go onto the mist or I don't. I live or I don't. There is no certainty but there never is."

"It doesn't distress you?"

"Of course it does. I love and I hate this bridge of yours. I will pine for the mist, for the need to cross it. But I do not want to be part of a family that all die young without even a corpse for the burning. If I have a child she will not need to make the decision I did: to cross the mist and die, or to stay safe on one side of the world and never see the other. She will lose something. She will gain something else."

"Do you hate me?" he said finally, afraid of the answer, afraid of any answer she might give.

"No. Oh, no." She rolled over to him and kissed his mouth, and Kit could not say if the salt he tasted was from her tears or his own.

The autumn was spent getting the chains across the river. In the days after the crossing, the rope was linked to another and pulled back the way it had come, coupled now; and then there were two ropes in parallel courses. It was tricky work, requiring careful communications via the signal towers, but it was completed without event, and Kit could at last get a good night's sleep. To break the rope would have been to start anew with the long difficult crossing. Over the next days, each rope was replaced with fishskin cable strong enough to take the weight of the chains until they were secured.

The cables were hoisted to the tops of the pillars, to prefigure the path one of the eight chains would take: secured with heavy pins set in protected slots in the anchorages, making straight sharp lines to the saddles on the pillars and then, two hundred feet above the mist, the long perfect catenary. A catwalk was suspended from the cables. For the first time, people could cross the mist without the boats, though few chose to do so, except for the high workers from the capital and the coast: a hundred men and women so strong and graceful that they seemed another species and kept mostly to themselves. They were directed by a woman Kit had worked with before, Feinlin. The high-workers took no surnames. Something about Feinlin reminded him of Rasali.

The weather grew colder and the days shorter, and Kit pushed hard to have the first two chains across before the winter rains began. There would be no heavy work once the ground got too wet to give sturdy purchase to the teams. Calculations to the contrary, Kit could not quite trust that cables, even fishskin cables, would survive the weight of those immense arcs through an entire winter—or that a Big One would not take one down in the unthinking throes of some great storm.

The eyebars that would make up the chain were ten feet long and required considerable manhandling to be linked with bolts larger than a man's forearm. The links became a chain, even more cumbersome. Winches pulled the chain's end up to the saddles and out onto the catwalk.

After this, the work became even more difficult and painstaking. Feinlin and her people moved individual eyebars and pins out onto the catwalks and joined them in place; a backbreaking dangerous task that had to be exactly synchronized with the work on the other side of the river so that the cable would not be stressed.

Most nights Kit worked into the darkness. When the moons were bright enough, he, the high-workers, and the bridgewrights would work in shifts, day and night.

He crossed the mist six more times that fall. The high-workers disliked having people on the catwalks but he was the architect, after all, so he crossed once that way, struggling with vertigo. After that he preferred the ferries. When he crossed with Valo, they talked exclusively about the bridge—Valo had decided to stay until the bridge was complete and the ferries finished, though his mind was already full of the capital—but the other times, when it was Rasali, they were silent, listening to the hiss of the V-shaped scull moving in the mist. His fear of the mist decreased with each day they came closer to the bridge's completion, though he couldn't say why this was.

When Kit did not work through the night and Rasali was on the same side of the mist, they spent their nights together, sometimes making love, at other times content to share drinks or play ninepins in The Deer's Hart's garden. Kit's proficiency surprised everyone but himself—he had been famous for his accuracy, back in Atyar. He and Rasali did not talk again about what she would do when the bridge was complete, or what he would do, for that matter.

The hard work was worth it. It was still warm enough that the iron didn't freeze the high-workers' hands on the day they placed the final bolt. The first chain was complete.

Though work was slow through the winter, it was a mild one, and the second and third chains were in place by spring. The others were completed by the end of the summer.

With the heavy work done, some of the workers returned to their home-places. More than half had taken the name Bridger or something similar. "We have changed things," Kit said to Jenner on one of his Nearside visits, just before Jenner left for his new work. "No," Jenner said: "*You* have changed things." Kit did not respond but held this close and thought of it sometimes with mingled pride and fear.

The workers who remained were all high-workers, people who did not mind crawling about on the suspension chains securing the support ropes. For the past two years, the ropemakers for hundreds of miles up- and downstream had been twisting, cabling, looping, and reweaving the fishskin cables that would support the road deck. Crates, each marked with the suspender's position in the bridge, stood in carefully sorted towers in the old sheep field.

Kit's work was now all paperwork, it seemed—so many invoices, so many reports for the capital—but he managed every day to watch the high-workers. Sometimes he climbed to the tops of the pillars and looked down into the mist and saw Rasali's or Valo's ferry, a shape like an open eye half-hidden in tendrils of blazing white or pale gray.

Kit lost one more worker, Tommer Bullkeeper, who climbed onto the catwalk for a drunken bet and fell, with a maniacal cry that changed into unbalanced laughter as he vanished into the mist. His wife wept in mixed anger and grief, and the townspeople wore ash-color, and the bridge continued. Rasali held Kit when he cried in his room at The Bitch. "Never mind," she said. "Tommer was a good person: a drunk but good to his sons and his wife, careful with animals. People have always died. The bridge doesn't change that."

The towns changed shape as Kit watched. Commercial envoys from every direction gathered. Some stayed in inns and homes. Others built small houses, shops, and warehouses. Many used the ferries and it became common for these people to tip Rasali or Valo lavishly—"in hopes I never ride with you again," they would say. Valo laughed and spent this money buying beer for his friends. The letter had come from University and he would begin his studies with the winter term, so he had many farewells to make. Rasali told no one, not even Kit, what she planned to do with hers.

Beginning in the spring of the project's fifth year, they attached the road deck. Wood planks wide enough for oxen two abreast were nailed together with iron stabilizer struts. The bridge was made of several hundred sections constructed on the worksites and then hauled out by workers. Each segment had farther to go before being placed and secured. The two towns celebrated all night the first time a Nearsider shouted from her side of the bridge and was saluted by Farsider cheers. In the lengthening evenings, it became a pastime for people to walk onto the bridge and lie belly-down at its end, and look into the mist so far below them. Sometimes dark shapes moved within it but no one saw anything big enough to be a Big One. A few heedless locals dropped heavy stones from above to watch the mist twist away, opening holes into its depths, but their neighbors stopped them. "It's not respectful," one said; and, "Do you want to piss them off?" said another.

Kit asked her but Rasali never walked out with him. "I see enough from the river," she said.

Kit was Nearside, in his room in The Fish. He had lived in this room for five years and it looked it. Plans and timetables overlapped one another, pinned to the walls in the order he had needed them. The chair by the fire was heaped with clothes, books, a length of red silk he had seen at a fair and could not resist. It had been years since he sat there. The plans in his folio and on the oversized table had been replaced with waybills and receipts for materials, payrolls, and copies of correspondence between Kit and his sponsors in the government. The window was open and Kit sat on the cupboard bed, watching a bee feel its way through the sun-filled air. He'd left half a pear on the table. He was waiting to see if the bee would find it, and thinking about the little hexagonal cells of a beehive, whether they were stronger than squares were and how he might test this.

Feet ran along the corridor. His door flew open. Rasali stood there blinking in the light, which was so golden that Kit didn't at first notice how pale she was, or the tears on her face. "What—" he said as he swung off his bed.

"Valo," she said. "*Pearlfinder*."

He held her. The bee left, then the sun, and still he held her as she rocked silently on the bed. Only when the square of sky in the window faded to purple and the little moon's crescent eased across it, did she speak. "Ah," she said, a sigh like a gasp. "I am so tired." She fell asleep as quickly as that, with tears still wet on her face. Kit slipped from the room.

The taproom was crowded, filled with ash-gray clothes, with soft voices and occasional sobs. Kit wondered for a moment if everyone had a set of mourning clothes always at hand and what this meant about them.

Brana Keep saw Kit in the doorway and came from behind the bar to speak with him. "How is she?" she said.

"I think she's asleep right now," Kit said. "Can you give me some food for her, something to drink?"

Brana nodded, spoke to her daughter Lixa as she passed into the back, then returned. "How are *you* doing, Kit? You saw a fair amount of Valo yourself."

"Yes," Kit said. Valo chasing the children through the field of stones, Valo laughing at the top of a tower, Valo serious-eyed with a handbook of the calculus in the shade of a half-built fishing boat. "What happened? She hasn't said anything yet."

Brana spread her hands out. "What can be said? Signal flags said he was going to cross just after midday but he never came. When we signaled over they said he left when they signaled."

"Could he be alive?" Kit asked, remembering the night that he and Rasali had lost the big scull, the extra hours it had taken for the crossing. "He might have broken the scull, landed somewhere downriver."

"No," Brana said. She was crying, too. "I know, that's what we wanted to hope. But Asa, one of the strangers, the high-workers; she was working overhead and heard the boat capsize, heard him cry out. She couldn't see anything and didn't know what she had heard until we figured it out."

"Three more months," Kit said mostly to himself. He saw Brana looking at him so he clarified: "Three more months. The bridge would have been done. This wouldn't have happened."

"This was today," Brana said, "not three months from now. People die when they die. We grieve and move on, Kit. You've been with us long enough to understand how we see these things. Here's the tray."

When Kit returned, Rasali was asleep. He watched her in the dark room, unwilling to light more than the single lamp he'd carried up with him. *People die when they die.* But he could not stop thinking about the bridge, the nearly finished deck. *Another three months. Another month.*

When she awakened, there was a moment when she smiled at him, her face weary but calm. Then she remembered and her face tightened and she started crying again. After a while Kit got her to eat some bread and fish and cheese and drink some watered wine. She did so obediently, like a child. When she was finished she lay back against him. Her matted hair pushed up into his mouth.

"How can he be gone?"

"I'm so sorry," Kit said. "The bridge was so close to finished. Three more months, and this wouldn't have—"

She pulled away. "What? Wouldn't have happened? Wouldn't have *had* to happen?" She stood and faced him. "His death would have been unnecessary?"

"I—" Kit began but she interrupted him, new tears streaking her face.

"He *died*, Kit. It wasn't necessary, it wasn't irrelevant, it wasn't anything except the way things are. But he's gone and I'm not and *now* what do I do, Kit? I lost my father and my aunt and my sister and my brother and my brother's son, and now I lose the mist when the bridge is done and then what? What am I then? Who are the Ferry people then?"

Kit knew the answer. However she changed, she would still be Rasali. Her people would still be strong and clever and beautiful. The mist would still be there, and the Big Ones. But she wouldn't be able to hear these words, not yet, not for months maybe. So he held her and let his own tears slip down his face and tried not to think.

Five years after the Oncalion bridge was completed, Kit was two years into building an aqueduct planned across the Bakyar valley. There were problems. The first stones could not sustain both the weight of the aqueduct and the water it was meant to carry. His predecessor on the project had been either incompetent or corrupt, and Kit was still sorting through the mess she had left behind. They were a season behind schedule, but when he heard about Davell Meinem's death, he left immediately for Atyar. Some time would be required to put his father's affairs in order but mostly he did not wish to miss Twentieth-day, when Davell would be remembered. Kit had known that Davell's death would leave a hole in him, but he had known his father was dying for years. He hadn't expected this to hurt as much as it did.

The Grayfield was a little amphitheatre Davell had designed when he was young, matured now to a warm half-circle of white stone and grass, fringed with cherry trees. It was a warm day, brilliantly sunny. The air smelled of honey-cakes and the last of the cherry blossoms. Kit was Davell's only child, so he stood alone at the red-tasseled archway to greet those who came. He was not surprised at how many came to honor his father, more and more until the amphitheatre overflowed, the honey-cakes were all eaten, and the silver bowls were filled with flowers, one from each mourner. Davell Meinem had built seven bridges, three aqueducts, a forum, two provincial complexes, and innumerable smaller projects, and he had maintained contacts with old friends from each of them; many more people had liked him for his humor and his kindness.

What surprised Kit was all the people who had come for *his* sake: fellow students, tutors, old lovers and companions, even the man who ran the wine shop he frequented whenever he was in the city. Many of them had never even met his father. He had not known that he was part of their patterns.

Five months later, when he was back in the Bakyar valley, a letter arrived wrapped in dirty oiled paper and clearly from far away. It was from the miners of Oncalion. "We heard about your father from a trader when we were asking about you," the letter said. "We are sorry for your loss."

The fairs to celebrate the opening of the bridge started days before the official date of Midsummer. Representatives of Empire, from Atyar and Triple, from the regional governors and anyone else who could contrive an excuse all polished their speeches and waited impatiently in suites of tents erected on hurriedly cleaned-up fields near (but not too near) Nearside. The town had bled northward until it surrounded the west pillar of the bridge. The land that had once been sheep-pasture—Sheepfield, it was now—at the foot of the pillar was crowded with fair tents and temporary booths, cheek by jowl with more permanent shops of wood and stone that sold food and the sorts of products a traveler might find herself needing.

Kit was proud of the new streets. He had organized construction of the crosshatch of sturdy cobblestones as something to do while he waited through the bridge's final year. The new wells had been a project of Jenner's, planned from the very beginning, but Kit had seen them completed. Kit had just received a letter from Jenner with news of his new mist bridge up in the Keitche mountains: on schedule, a happy work site. It was gneiss bedrock, so he was using explosives and had hired Liu Breaker for it; she was there now and sent her greetings.

Kit walked alone through the fair which had climbed the levee and established itself along the ridge. A few people, townspeople and workers, greeted him but others only pointed him out to their friends (*the man who built the bridge; see there, that short dark man*); and still others ignored him completely, just another stranger in a crowd of strangers. When he had first come to build the bridge everyone in Nearside knew everyone else, local or visitor. He felt solitude settling around him again, the loneliness of coming to a strange place and building something and then leaving. The people of Nearside were moving forward into this new world he had built, the world of a bridge across the mist, but he was not going with them.

He wondered what Rasali was doing over in Farside, and wished he could see her. They had not spoken since the days after Valo's death except once for a few minutes when he had come upon her at The Bitch. She had been withdrawn though not hostile. He had felt unbalanced and not sought her out since.

Now, at the end of his great labor, he longed to see her. When would she cross next? He laughed. He of all people should know better: *ten minutes' walk*.

The bridge was not yet officially open but Kit was the architect. The guards at the toll booth only nodded when he asked to pass and lifted the gate for him. A few people noticed and gestured as he climbed. When Uni Mason (hands filled with fairings) shouted something he could not hear clearly, Kit smiled and waved and walked on.

He had crossed the bridge before this. The first stage of building the heavy oak frames that underlay the roadbed had been a narrow strip of planking that led from one shore to the other. Nearly every worker had found some excuse for crossing it at least once before Empire had sent people to the tollgates. Swallowing his fear of the height, Kit himself had crossed it nearly every day for the last two months.

This was different. It was no longer his bridge but belonged to Empire and to the people of Nearside and Farside. He saw it with the eyes of a stranger.

The stone ramp was a quarter of a mile long, inclined gradually for carts. Kit hiked up, and the noises dropped behind and below him. The barriers that would keep animals (and people) from seeing the drop-off to either side were not yet complete: there were always things left unfinished at a bridge's opening, afterthoughts and additions. Ahead of him, the bridge was a series of perfect dark lines and arcs.

The ramp widened as it approached the pillar, and offered enough space for a cart to carefully turn onto the bridge itself. The bed of the span was barely wide enough for a cart with two oxen abreast, so Nearside and Farside would have to take turns sending wagons across. *For now,* Kit thought. *Later we can widen it, or build another. They.* It would be someone else.

The sky was overcast with high clouds the color of tin, their metallic sheen reflected in the mist below Kit. There were no railings, only fishskin ropes strung between the suspension cables that led up to the chains. Oxen and horses wouldn't like that, or the hollow sound their feet would make on the boards. Kit watched the deck roll before him in the wind, which was constant from the southwest. The roll wasn't so bad in this wind but perhaps they should add an iron railing or more trusses to lessen the twisting and make crossing more comfortable. Empire had sent a new engineer to take care of any final projects: Jeje Tesanthe at Atyar. He would mention it to her.

Kit walked to one side so that he could look down. Sound dropped off behind him, deadened as it always was by the mist. He could almost imagine that he was alone. It was several hundred feet down, but there was nothing to give scale to the coiling field of hammered metal below him. Deep in the mist he saw shadows that might have been a Big One or something smaller or a thickening of the mist, and then, his eyes learning what to look for, he saw more of the shadows, as though a school of fish were down there. One separated and darkened as it rose in the mist until it exposed its back almost immediately below Kit.

It was dark and knobby, shiny with moisture, flat as a skate, and it went on forever—thirty feet long perhaps, or forty, twisting as it rose to expose its underside or what he thought might be its underside. As Kit watched, the mist curled back from a flexing scaled wing of sorts, and then a patch that might have been a single eye or a field of eyes or something altogether different, and then a mouth like the arc of the suspension chains. The mouth gaped open to show another arc, a curve of gum or cartilage. The creature rolled and then sank and became a shadow and then nothing as the mist closed back over it.

Kit had stopped walking when he saw it. He forced himself to move forward again. A Big One, or perhaps just a Medium-Large One. At this height it hadn't seemed so big or so frightening. Kit was surprised at the sadness he felt.

Farside was crammed with color and fairings as well, but Kit could not find Rasali anywhere. He bought a tankard of rye beer and went to find some place alone.

Once it became dark and the Imperial representatives were safely tucked away for the night, the guards relaxed the rules and let their friends—and then any of the locals—on the bridge to look around. People who had worked on the bridge had papers to cross without charge for the rest of their lives but many others had watched it grow, and now they charmed or bribed or begged their way onto their bridge. Covered lamps were permitted, though torches were forbidden because of the oil that protected the fishskin ropes. From his seat on the levee, Kit watched the lights move along the bridge, there and then hidden by the suspension cables and deck, dim and inconstant as fireflies.

"Kit Meinem of Atyar."

Kit stood and turned to the voice behind him. "Rasali Ferry of Farside." She wore blue and white, and her feet were bare. She had pulled back her dark hair with a ribbon and her pale shoulders gleamed. She glowed under the moonlight like mist. He thought of touching her, kissing her, but they had not spoken since just after Valo's death.

She stepped forward and took the mug from his hand, drank the lukewarm beer, and just like that the world righted itself. He closed his eyes and let the feeling wash over him.

He took her hand and they sat on the cold grass and looked out across the river. The bridge was a black net of arcs and lines. Behind it the mist glowed blue-white in the light of the moons. After a moment he asked, "Are you still Rasali Ferry, or will you take a new name?"

"I expect I'll take a new one." She half-turned in his arms so that he could see her face, her eyes. "And you? Are you still Kit Meinem, or do you become someone else? Kit Who Bridged the Mist? Kit Who Changed the World?"

"Names in the city do not mean the same thing," Kit said absently. "*Did* I change the world?" He knew the answer already.

She looked at him for a moment as though trying to gauge his feelings. "Yes," she said slowly after a moment. She turned her face up toward the loose strand of bobbing lights: "There's your proof, as permanent as stone and sky."

"'Permanent as stone and sky,'" Kit repeated. "This afternoon—it flexes a lot, the bridge. There has to be a way to control it but it's not engineered for that yet. Or lightning could strike it. There are a thousand things that could destroy it. It's going to come down, Rasali. This year, next year, a hundred years from now, five hundred." He ran his fingers through his hair. "All these people, they think it's forever."

"No, we don't," Rasali said. "Maybe Atyar does, but we know better here. Do you need to tell a Ferry that nothing will last? *These* cables will fail eventually, *these* stones will fall—but not the *dream* of crossing the mist, the dream of connection. Now that we know it can happen, it will always be here. My father died. My sister Rothiel. My brother Ster. Valo." She stopped, swallowed. "Ferrys die, but there is always a Ferry to cross the mist. Bridges and ferryfolk, they are not so different, Kit." She leaned forward, across the space between them, and they kissed.

"Are you off soon?"

Rasali and Kit had made love on the levee against the cold grass. They had crossed the bridge together under the sinking moons, walked back to The Deer's Hart and bought more beer, the crowds thinner now, people gone home with their families or friends or lovers—the strangers from out of town bedding down in spare rooms, tents, anywhere they could. But Kit was too restless to sleep and he and Rasali ended up back by the mist, down on the dock. Morning was only a few hours away and the smaller moon had set. It was darker now and the mist had dimmed.

"In a few days," Kit said, thinking of the trunks and bags packed tight and gathered in his room at The Fish: the portfolio, fatter now and stained with water, mist, dirt and sweat. Maybe it was time for a new one. "Back to the capital."

There were lights on the opposite bank, fishers preparing for their work despite the fair, the bridge. *Some things don't change.*

"Ah," she said. They both had known this. It was no surprise. "What will you do there?"

Kit rubbed his face and felt stubble under his fingers. "Sleep for a hundred years. Then there's another bridge they want, down at the mouth of the river, a place called Ulei. The mist's nearly a mile wide. I'll go down and look at the site and start working on a budget."

"A mile," Rasali said. "Can you do it?"

"I think so. I bridged this, didn't I?" His gesture took in the bridge and the woman beside him. "Ulei is on an alluvial plain. There are some low islands. That's the only reason it's possible. So maybe a series of flat stone arches, one to the next. You? You'll keep building boats?"

"No." She leaned her head back and he felt her face against his ear. She smelled sweet and salty. "I don't need to. I have a lot of money. The rest of the family can build boats but for me that was just what I did while I waited to cross the mist again."

"You'll miss it," Kit said. It was not a question.

Her strong hand laid over his. "Mmm," she said, a sound without implication.

"But it was the *crossing* that mattered to you," Kit said, realizing it. "Just as with me, but in a different way."

"Yes," she said and after a pause: "So now I'm wondering. How big do the Big Ones get in the Mist Ocean? And what's on the other side?"

"Nothing's on the other side," Kit said. "There's no crossing something without an end."

"Everything can be crossed. Of course it has an end. There's a river of water deep under the Mist River, yes? And that water runs somewhere. And all the other rivers, all the lakes—they all drain somewhere. There's a water ocean under the Mist Ocean and I wonder whether the mist ends somewhere out there, if it spreads out and vanishes and you find you are floating on water."

"It's a different element," Kit said, turning the problem over. "So you would need a boat that works through mist, light enough with that broad belly and fishskin sheathing; but it would have to be deep-keeled enough for water."

She nodded. "I want to take a coast-skimmer and refit it, find out what's out there. Islands, Kit. Big Ones. *Huge* Ones. Another whole world maybe. I think I would like to be Rasali Ocean."

"You will come to Ulei with me?" he said but he knew already. She *would* come, for a month or a season or a year or even longer, perhaps. They would sleep tumbled together in an inn very like The Fish or The Bitch, and when her boat was finished, she would sail across Ocean, and he would move on to the next bridge or road. Or he might return to the capital and a position at University. Or he might rest at last.

"I will come," she said. "For a bit."

Suddenly he felt a deep and powerful emotion in his chest: overwhelmed by everything that had happened or would happen in their lives, the changes to Nearside and Farside, the ferry's ending, Valo's death, the fact that she would leave him eventually or that he would leave her. "I'm sorry," he said.

"I'm not," she said and leaned across to kiss him, her mouth warm with sunlight and life. "It is worth it, all of it."

All those losses, but this one at least he could prevent.

"When the time comes," he said: "When you sail. I will come with you,"

A fo ben, bid bont. To be a leader, be a bridge.
—*Welsh proverb*

www.ingramcontent.com/pod-product-compliance
Lightning Source LLC
Chambersburg PA
CBHW030336310726
48979CB00001B/55

* 9 7 8 1 6 4 9 7 3 0 3 1 2 *